"You look perfec  mean mostly uninju tiny hand over her ey

Feeling braver t gently remove the ha ...d hold it to my own. "See, I'm fine, ...isper as I gently rub my thumb over her tiny knuckles.

Her eyes lift to mine and lock our gazes. I have always found the golden color of her eyes fascinating but never studied them up close. They are light brown with a golden star in the middle. I am literally star ⁓ gazing as she takes in the injuries to my face. We stand there for about a minute, lost in time.

I wonder if she is thinking about when we first started dating, the hard times that followed, the present, or the future. I search her face for clues but don't want to break the spell by opening my mouth. I decide to put said mouth to better use by lowering my head toward hers.

To Renee,
Welcome to
Strawberry!
♡
Marilyn
Barr

Bear with Me

by

Marilyn Barr

Strawberry Shifters, Book 1

Bear with Me

Cover Art by *Tina Lynn Stout*

The Wild Rose Press, Inc.
PO Box 708
Adams Basin, NY 14410-0708
Visit us at www.thewildrosepress.com

Publishing History
First Black Rose Edition, 2020
Print ISBN 978-1-5092-3136-2
Digital ISBN 978-1-5092-3137-9

Strawberry Shifters, Book 1
Published in the United States of America

Dedication

To my own grouchy bear—
thank you for always finding me fascinating
and building a fairytale life where I can be myself

Chapter 1

Gazing over my garden, I feel a deluge of sadness. Plants have been uprooted for three weeks awaiting our big move to a castle in a small town. Wiping a tear, I remind myself to feel grateful our destination is Kentucky. They do not have any limitations on plants crossing over state lines or quarantine policies. My little darlings will be in the back of the truck tomorrow morning and quickly replanted after enduring five hours of my driving. The fact we will not be separated is the only piece keeping my anxiety at bay. I depend on these plants to provide sensory relief that my body cannot produce on its own.

"There, there, little sage," I coo as I place my fingers in the soil around a wilting plant. The plant not only perks up, but little neophytes emerge in a ring around it. *Oops.* I look over my shoulders to see if anyone noticed my magic. I've been able to make plants grow by touching them my whole life but choose to keep it a secret from the world. Having sensory processing disorder put me under the microscope as a kid.

The last thing I need is for suburbia to find out I have magical powers too. Growing up, I begged my parents to let me live with my aunt who read tarot cards as a witch to tourists, but they refused. They wanted me to have a normal life. If only it wasn't so hard to be normal.

By some good fortune, I made it to college where I met Grant. I studied botany which allowed me to spend most of my time in the university greenhouse. Having a place where I could block out the sounds and smells of living on campus, was paramount to my decision on where to study. It was in the greenhouse, where Grant fell off a ladder and into my life. From the moment I looked into his deep blue eyes, I knew we were meant to be. Passion sparked immediately and after only a few months I found out I was pregnant with our son, Henrik.

Grant is not just a pair of pretty eyes though. My parents started calling him ultra-responsible after he asked to marry me, even though we hadn't been together long enough to forge a strong bond. Until our son was in kindergarten, it was our parents' idea to sacrifice living together so Grant could launch his career. I never finished my botany degree because long lab-based classes and newborn babies do not mix. However, I found my way and eventually got a job teaching classes at a garden center, which I truly enjoy.

Now I am leaving my job to follow Grant in a last-ditch attempt to make our marriage work. The initial passion between us has gone dormant from all the years apart, compounded from the struggles of moving in together with a family already in place. Grant works tirelessly to climb the pharmaceutical business ladder, trying to save the world with each new drug at each new company. However, his drive keeps him at work from dawn until dusk seven days a week, causing even more discord in our family.

To ease some of the tension between us and scout

out our new life, Grant moved to Strawberry, Kentucky ten months ago. Even today when the relocation company is unloading our belongings in our new home, no one is there to supervise because Grant has an FDA response letter that must be addressed. Tomorrow Henrik and I will bring the plants and sort through the chaos left in their wake.

As if on cue, I'm pulled from my thoughts by the slam of our back door. Henrik, now twelve years old, steps out into the garden to put his arms around me. "I know you don't want to move but thank you for taking me away from here," he says. His beaming smile is framed by two small dimples and shaggy light brown hair. Blue eyes highlighted with a yellow star surrounding their pupils crinkle at the edges in the same manner as his father's eyes.

"You are just looking forward to being homeschooled. When I withdrew you today, the principal called me into his office to talk about your behavior again. He thought I was removing you, so we didn't have to deal with all the disciplinary actions. I had to assure him we were moving to a town so small that the local school was an hour away." I frown at my son. Pulling him out to homeschool in another state is the best news Henrik's heard all year. I hand him some newspaper to help me wrap the tops of the plants for the ride in the morning.

"I couldn't help drumming on the desk, Mom. I had a melody in my head, and I needed to compose the song for it. I couldn't hear myself think with my math teacher talking. Then he called my songs a waste of time. Do you believe that?" he asks, accepting the paper from my hands to get to work. Despite his problems at school, he has always been helpful around the house. Homeschooling may as well be his best fit, as his need for a sensory reset comes from my genetics. Music helps him calm his senses the way the earth calms mine.

"In the context of math class, your songs are a waste of time. You must learn a whole math book before the state tests which are your gateway to a conservatory of music. Better grades would get you to a school with more music classes. However, we couldn't get you into a specialized school with your disciplinary status. Did you really need to yell at the teacher?" I ask in response. I give him a stern look and he has the grace to look sheepish. However, his impish smile tells me his remorse is all for show. *Little Dickens*.

"He threw my song in the trash! Besides my disciplinary record doesn't matter now that you are my teacher. I like how you teach math. You taught fractions using notes in a measure instead of pizzas. How many pizzas need to be cut in a day and who spends time measuring each piece?" He says throwing his arms in the air.

I must laugh at my precocious son. His ambition to fulfill his dream of becoming a composer comes from his father. Not that Grant can carry a tune in a bucket but the two of them bulldoze anyone in their way of success. This has been celebrated by pharmaceutical industries recruiting Grant. Too bad Henrik, as just a kid, has only met condemnation and opposition in public schools. It was Grant's idea to homeschool him, citing Henrik's need for focused education as his main reason.

However, the more Grant talked about it, the more

I got the feeling he was trying to accommodate my disorder by isolating us. If only he paid attention to my work at the garden center. I have created an environment where I can add to society without melting down in sensory overload.

The whole idea to move came when Grant got that sparkle, a few months ago. His dancing blue eyes told me he'd been contacted by a company that wanted to steal him from his current job. The potential employers dazzled my husband with ideas for a new life-saving drug over lunch at some fancy restaurant again. This will be his fifth job move in eight years. Grant's resume looks like he's a reprobate but each company offers considerably more money than the previous one so he must be doing something right. However, I would be the last to know because he's never home.

"It's our adventure, Henrik. We can make of it whatever we please. However, one thing is set in stone. You are going to spend more time in the fresh air and sunshine. I had materials delivered to the new house. Together we will build raised beds, hoop houses, and even mini-greenhouses. You need to work more of your body than just your ears." I try to sound excited. When I fail miserably, Henrik hugs me for the second time in this conversation. My little tough guy hasn't let me hug him in days.

"Yes, surprises and adventure around every corner! Unbridled Kentucky is awaiting your participation!" rumbles a masculine voice. The backdoor slams and Grant's footsteps thunder into the garden. Grant is not a tall man, but his presence makes him larger than life. My heart skips a beat as his voice projects across the garden. Between the caress of the sound waves and the vibrations of his footsteps, I am swept away in the sensations he brings. My heightened senses are delighted every time he is near, whether we are getting along or not.

Grant holds his hand out which Henrik takes to be lifted to his feet. My heart is warmed by the macho embrace between father and son. No matter how rocky our marriage has been, Henrik and Grant have always been close. I guess it's the mutual respect between two men who focus on the job at hand rather than the people around them.

"You're here. What happened to your call with the FDA, the response letter, and the crisis?" I ask cautiously. Had Grant come back to finish the fight we had over the phone last night or to help with tomorrow? Was this job losing its allure before I even move there?

"The piano movers needed my signature to put it in the blindingly hot pink bedroom. So, I left work and took the call on the Bluetooth system in the new car. I thought Bergan Pharma would appreciate my using their signing gift as a tool in their interests. Since I had time on my hands, I thought I would come up to show Henrik the photo of the piano settled in his new room. There's still time to pick a room that isn't hot pink." Grant holds out his phone for Henrik. Henrik grabs the phone out of his hands and squeals in delight. Having a piano in his room was a signing bonus for Henrik, not that he needed more enticement to move away.

"I picked up Chinese food on the way as well. There's not a Chinese restaurant within an hour of Strawberry, so I thought it would be an excellent farewell to city life. I also guessed your mother would lose track of time out here and forget about feeding our growing boy," Grant continues. That's Grant, I think to myself, always providing structure. Somehow, I find it more comforting than controlling. Henrik pumps his fist in the air with a cheer and runs into the house.

"I know you didn't come up here to show Henrik a picture you could have sent me through text. What brought you back?" I ask as soon as I hear the back door shut.

"I came back to apologize for our argument on the phone last night," Grant says quietly. "I got really nasty. I was worried you were backing out of the move because you couldn't fathom life without your safety net. I want you to believe I can create another safety net for you. I want to give you a castle filled with riches, far away from anything that stresses you. There are walls of windows in our new home, so you don't have to use the overhead lights that bother you. Henrik has multiple keyboards to fill the house with music to drown out any mechanical noises.

"You don't need to search for a job you can tolerate. I'm making enough money for you to stay home in riches, dripping in jewels." Despite being dressed in business clothes, Grant sits in the grass beside me. He picks up the paper Henrik had been using to continue wrapping plants.

I look down. My bare feet are caked in dirt. The dirt acts like thigh-high tights hiding my skin until it passes the job to my ancient shorts and top. Sleeves made of dirt and grime end in short ragged fingernails. I do not need to question whether there is mud on my face but rather where on my face the mud might have missed. How can he look at my happy, muddy face and offer me riches and jewels? It's like his vision is filtered so he can't see the real me.

"Thank you, and I'm sorry too. I want to start over as much as you do. I promise. The fact you came back to apologize shows me you are committed to changing. I'm optimistic. We can work this out," I say quietly.

"We will work it out," Grant declares, "because I really want this." He puts his arm out as if to put it around my shoulders only to stop midway. He drops it to his side abruptly and I wonder what he means by this. I'm too afraid of his response to ask if he is referring to us sharing a bedroom again after five years of self-imposed exile.

His features soften as we stare at each other. I search his face for some sign of love. Beyond his honor, is there a glimmer of true affection for me? I ask myself over and over if he loves me. The most pathetic part is how much I still love him. I burn for him, even now when we are failing to communicate. I wonder what would happen if I kissed him out of the blue. Would he let me kiss him out of duty, push me away, or kiss me back? I can't remember our last kiss, but I remember the passionate ones in the beginning. I would do anything to see that hunger return to his eyes.

Chapter 2

"White pizza, black olives"; my wife's voice warms the inside of my car. My signing bonus, this sleek black AWD BMW, hugs the curves and hills of Kentucky like a dream. The slight drizzle and dropping temperatures would spell disaster for the old car I left in Ohio. The new car is one of the many perks required to uproot my household, but to me, it has been worth it. I would do anything to make our new life work, even if it means bringing home pizza every Friday night and staying in with my family.

"No problem," I say leaning slightly into the speaker. I'll get used to the blue tooth speakers...someday. Truth be told I had placed the order ten minutes before she called. Not that I'm clairvoyant, but I promised my wife I would start listening to her when we moved. I found she often asks for the same things repeatedly, which makes me wonder how I managed to mess up so often in our old life.

She only asked me to listen. I, on the other hand, asked her to quit her job, leave her family and friends, and move to a state she had only seen on TV. Due to her disorder, she's rigid in many ways. I have been happily surprised at her amiable attitude in the whirlwind of all this change. It's not easy to move from a capital city to a country town even for the most flexible of people.

The two-stoplight town of Strawberry is home to Josh's Auto and Gas depot, Ray's Market, Paulino's Pizza, a chiropractor's office, and little else. The little town recently started booming for two large reasons: the first is the giant plantation homes for pennies on the dollar and second is its proximity to Bergan Pharma. Bergan Pharma exploded into the market three years ago with a miracle product to fix gut dysbiosis. The whole company runs twenty-four hours a day, not just medicine production, doing business around the world. Overnight, they went from unknown to market leader seemingly by magic.

It had been an early Christmas present when the head-hunter called me about Bergan Pharma. They needed someone to get their products approved by the FDA, which is my specialty. You could say I possess a certain set of skills coveted by the industry, but less James Bond and more Bob Cratchit. Up until that call, I hopped from one slave driver to the next. Every company promised innovations but really, they were all the same.

First, a trust-fund kid parties through undergrad who uses a nerdy "friend" to barely slide through with a degree in something dumb like underwater basket weaving. Next, they build a start-up pharma company and the nerdy friend drives a group of employees into the ground for the success of "their" invention. Finally, the partners have a happily ever after of saving a little slice of the world while making the big bucks.

They marry and have kids to start the cycle over. It's my job to make all the bar napkins, lab books, scrap paper musings, and alcohol-fueled business models into a cohesive professional package. Sometimes I am assigned a minion to help me, like a blue-haired neighbor or barely legal "friend" of the boss to manage the dozen boulder-sized binders.

I have over forty New Drug Applications—miracle-working piles of binders otherwise known as NDAs—somewhere in the FDA pipeline. They have been filed with five different companies. My name is all over their site as a name for inquiries only, never profit share. My bosses have always obliged with a signature for that part.

As I pull up to Paulino's Pizza, I am happy I called ahead. The line has reached the entrance with two IT specialists from Bergan holding the door. Nate and James had been in my office thirty minutes ago. The two loveable slackers live together, work together, game together, and apparently, they eat pizza together on Friday night with everyone else in town.

Their giant frames occupy my office guest chairs several times a day like a set of department store bookends. Not that they look alike. Nate looks like a pale movie villain while James is dark-skinned like an Italian, Spaniard, or Greek. With a last name like Martin, his nationality is anyone's guess. Currently, they look like overpaid bouncers holding the door in the dilapidated strip mall.

"Moonlighting, are we?" I call.

"Uh sir, we can't let you in dressed like that. We have standards to uphold," Nate retorts as I approach the shop tucked between Beula's salon and Dr. Van Dijk's office.

"Yeah, no workaholics allowed," James laughs while tugging my tie and swatting my hair.

"Hey now, that's my disguise. I have to at least look like I'm an executive director," I quip. Our mild shoving match ends abruptly when I hear my name squawked from inside.

"Sorry guys, R.H.I.P.," I say with a wink as I step ahead of my cohorts.

"It's only because you called ahead," calls James after me. I acknowledge the comment with a smirk while tapping my temple, which is rewarded with single finger salutes.

Paulino's Pizza can only be described as a diamond in the rough. The unlit sign on the crumbling storefront sits above the door. Inside arises a gauntlet created by two six-foot walls decorated with Paulino family photos. Some of the photos are so old they are sporting horse-drawn buggies in sepia coloring. At the end of the gauntlet, is a sign that reads "hostess seats you, do not seat yourself" in bold angry letters. Just behind the hospitality sign is a tall counter with an analog register shielding a bustling kitchen.

To the right of the kitchen, is a small dining room with red-checked plastic table clothes and barely audible Frank Sinatra music customary to American pizza joints. Three identical teenage guys are buzzing from table to table like bees carrying giant pizzas, soda pitchers, and empty plates. Behind the archaic register, are younger clones of the guys in the dining room. Manning the pasta roller and pizza oven are the smallest sons of the owner, Rosie Paulino.

"Grant, quit playing and get this home to your darling wife. Her basil has made my new pesto sauce a hit! How does she get it to grow so well in November?" snaps Rosie, the black slash undulating across her forehead with each syllable. At barely over four feet tall, Rosie Paulino's booming voice gives her the stature lacking in her bones. Running the community hang out and raising six boys alone would have overwhelmed anyone else. However, she manages it with grit to spare, which she uses to micromanage anyone who enters her domain.

As I squeeze between the hospitality sign and the line of hungry diners, I hear Rosie harangue me again. "Really Grant, did you travel from Siberia to get here? Do you need a rest from your long journey?"

I have the sense to look sheepish and apologize. Unfortunately, son #4 by the pizza oven is dumb enough to snicker with a volume Rosie can hear. The silent Mrs. Paulino Sr., mother-in-law to Rosie but Gran to everyone else, dressing salads in a dainty chair whacks him on the back of the head. I wince at the "*crack*" that follows but Rosie doesn't even flinch.

"I put cups of the sauce on the side because I know that is how Alison eats it. You can tell she's only half Italian. There's the red, pink, green in the cups while a new aioli is on the pie. It's so garlicky, it is a vampire repellent." Rosie winks at the last remark while accepting my credit card.

"Thank you so much. I'm sure she will love it," I reply hastily and head for the door. I grab my pizza and turn to the crowd of hungry diners still in line. Forlorn faces gaze back with tongues flashing to lick their frowning mouths. I squeeze past them and past my wayward colleagues still holding the door. By now the line is down the sidewalk blocking the chiropractor's office door. The pizzeria is only open for dinner and only four nights a week, but that is more Rosie's choice than lack of customers. Perhaps there is a deal between the two businesses as the chiropractor is always closed when Paulino's is open.

I take a picture of the pizza and send it to Alison when I get back to the car. Opening the sunroof, I fly through the woods south of Strawberry. I put the machine in sport mode to enjoy all 258 foot-pounds of torque traveling past the late autumn trees. My wide tires grip the curves of the rural roads and I am relieved it is still too warm for ice to form on them.

Flashes of gold, reds, oranges, and browns follow me to the long driveway of my home. Looking at the clock, I decide to hold the box open as I enter our home. She will be more likely to excuse my late arrival if I'm carrying treasure.

Chapter 3

"Breathe in; breathe out," I say to the floor-to-ceiling windows. I love these windows. Their admittance of ambient light allows me to keep the noisy candescent lights off for most of the day. The windows make me feel free and safe at the same time. As I sit in a lotus before them, my senses are tranquil. I am safe from the rioting stimuli of the modern world that constantly assault me. I desperately try to absorb the calm and center myself.

I focus on the soft piano music drifting through the house. It is another serene masterpiece by Henrik. This song sounds slightly melancholy, matching the gray weather out of the windows. I slow my heart rate to the tempo of the music with deep healing breaths. Today I stretched myself beyond my comfort zone with Henrik's help, and now I must recover before Grant comes home.

While I am in love with the natural light touching every corner of the house, Henrik loves our new home for a different reason. The upstairs has ten rooms, but vaulted ceilings are in the farthest suite from the master suite. I'll never forget his face the first time he stepped into his gaudy room. He walked to the center, sang a few notes and smiled at the ceiling. Both of us have an exaggerated sense of hearing so I was fortunate to share the echo of the notes bouncing from the walls to the ceiling and back down. Henrik declared it his space and lobbied to buy the house. Grant tried to talk Henrik out of living in a magenta bedroom several times to no avail.

Henrik does not routinely ask for things like most boys, so I made it my mission to paint that bedroom. His room is his creative space where he spends most of his waking hours living up to his label of a virtuoso. Time flies for him as he learns how to compose music and write screenplays. I help him sign up for online classes and then leave him alone to create until he needs to eat, sleep, or socialize.

This means today we had a ninety-minute drive to the big box hardware store in the closest suburb of Louisville. Even though our new town is too small to warrant a hardware store of its own, I wanted to take Henrik to a store with hundreds of shades to paint his room.

The plan was to get the paint today, which we did; get Grant to help paint it tomorrow; and then have the room ready for an electrician to come on Monday to install an intercom system between Henrik's room, the master suite, and the kitchen.

My mental wanderings give way to panic as I ponder what might be keeping my husband. My mind envisions the worst: car accident, a bombing at Paulino's pizza, or alien abduction. Then my thoughts turn more sinister like a stop for "one drink with the guys" getting out of hand. I give a slap to my errant thoughts. Over the course of our marriage, I have devoured every marriage manual I could set my hands upon.

"Have faith. Respect his boundaries. Trust him," I

chant against the music. I promised I would be all-in if we moved to Kentucky together. I must keep my part of the bargain.

The rumble of the garage door brings me out of my meditation. Henrik's music instantly stops as he too feels the vibrations. I hear a car door slam, heavy footsteps, and the beep of our security system disengaging. A bubble of anticipation inflates under my ribs while butterflies take flight in my abdomen. As the door opens, I am teased by the smell of Italian food, cologne, and Grant.

My senses filter out the spicy-sweet scent, unique to my husband's skin. The hairs on my arm stand on end as electricity crackles between us. We have yet to acknowledge each other but my body and soul go on alert at his presence.

"Hey Dad," Henrik says, locking forearms with Grant.

"Hey, how's my castle guard? Are you keeping our queen safe?"

"Oh Dad, she's the grown-up and I'm the kid. We took a road trip all the way to Louisville today. We listened to the alternative station on the radio, ate burritos, and got russet brown paint for my room. It was killer," Henrik babbles excitedly.

"Killer, huh? How did your mother manage on this killer trip?" I hear Grant ask cautiously. From my spot on the floor, I can't see them. However, I can imagine Grant's eyebrow quirked and his frown severe.

This is confirmed by Henrik's reply: "Don't make that worried face, Dad. I was by her side the whole time."

When had I become a burden to be watched? How

fragile do they think I am? This is a big part of our marriage problems: Grant doesn't see me as a partner but as a dependent. Power surges through my legs as my building fury boosts me from my lotus position to standing. Two heads, adorned with matching frowns, snap toward my direction.

"We are fine. We went to the hardware store not Mars. Really, Grant, I did reach adulthood before I met you," I blast at him. Even though I'm angry at his interrogation of Henrik, I'm struck dumb coming face-to-face with him. He runs his fingers through his shaggy brown hair and my fingers itch to do the same. I watch the thick strands fall back in place over his forehead with yearning. Impossibly long lashes frame blue eyes that are crinkled at the edges in amusement.

The laughter I see in them cools my temper and puts me at ease. This is what I love most about Grant. When my senses or my temper go riotous, he provides security, grounding, and structure. His chosen boundaries for my life are smaller than I would like, but it is better than floating in the wind. If only we could find a balance between white knight protector and absentee husband...

My eyes take on a life of their own and are compelled to drift downward over his body. His tie hangs loosely from around his open collar as if he has torn himself free from his work persona on the drive home. His arms are folded over his chest, hiding his long fingers and graceful hands. However, his rolled sleeves let me peek at his forearms lightly adorned with coarse hairs. I'm still staring at his arms when he holds up his hands to placate me.

"I worry, that's all. What if you get an anxiety

attack? You would be helpless and hours away. I wouldn't even know you needed me or where you were," he says in a soothing voice. I was taking in his appearance and lost the thread of the conversation. I feel myself start to blush at my loss of words.

Luckily, Henrik chimes in. "Mom was fine. She only had a problem with fluorescent lights in the store. I gave her my earbuds to cover up the squeals of the lights and I handled the salespeople. You would have been proud of me."

The fire inside me dampens as it is replaced by love for our son. He was my hero today. We were able to take our little adventure because Henrik was at my side when I needed him. Why can't Grant take that tactic? He should be at my side, in case I need him, trying new things instead of locking me in a palace where I can't find trouble.

"It's not like I get heart attacks or seizures that spontaneously incapacitate me. I have triggers which we all know. I also have tricks to help me cope, like Henrik's quick thinking with his earbuds. Having sensory processing disorder doesn't make me any less capable than you," I ruffle Henrik's hair as I praise him, and he shares a secret grin with me.

"Let's eat so Henrik and I can move furniture tonight," Grant says opening the bounty from Paulino's, signaling the end of this discussion like shutting a book. "Rosie made a DIY meal for us so you could do something with the sauces. She said you would know all about it. Oh, and she really appreciates the herbs you have been bringing over."

"We can't paint his room tonight. It's getting late and we won't have enough light. Let's spend the day painting together tomorrow," I plead. I hate that I sound like I'm begging for time with him. Grant tends to spend every waking hour at the office no matter which company he is employed. He takes on each submission like a personal vendetta.

"Tomorrow I'm going into the office to write some of the submission pieces. With fewer staff members, there will be fewer interruptions. I'm so close to sending it out and it will be my first big win for Bergan," Grant states. His statement is welcomed by Henrik's sour face.

"Mom, why can't you and I paint tomorrow? Dad and I can move furniture tonight and tomorrow night when the paint dries," Henrik asks.

"Because the ladders that go up to the ceiling are too tall for you to maneuver. Please don't try it. One of you will fall off a ladder, get crushed by a ladder falling, or find some way to get hurt," Grant counters.

I'm going to let Henrik take over this battle. Both of them have talked to me about the magenta room and I have provided a solution. They need to work out the scheduling. It's amusing to watch two men so alike fight over a common goal. I begin to sort the contents of my plate. My disorder magnifies food textures so small pieces like rice, grated vegetables or in this case pizza crust pieces need to be eaten separately.

They brush along my gums like sandpaper. The sorting absorbs my attention, being extra cautious so I don't accidentally get scratched. I divide each pizza slice into bite-sized pieces and sort them before blobs of sauces.

I feel Grant watching me and am instantly self-conscious. My eyes lift to him as their conversation stops. A flaming blush creeps to my cheeks. He looks mesmerized watching me. Embarrassment fades away at his acceptance. My small hands flutter into my lap. The delicate actions, required before I eat, have always fascinated him. However, he has never asked me about them or judged me in any way.

We exchange a small smile. I watch him swallow and start to reach in my direction. At the last minute, he seems to catch the action and withdraws to start eating.

Breaking the spell, Henrik shares another suggestion with a frown. "Why can't Dad and I paint overnight?"

"Your father has important work to do tomorrow. We can't have him writing gibberish because we are excited to paint your room. We are depending on him to fund our household."

"I'm not teaching at the garden center anymore. How about you two move furniture tonight so you and I can paint the lower half tomorrow? Then when your dad gets home, we will paint the top half while you sleep in the guest room. You will wake up to a russet brown room."

Whether it is the offer I provide or the tone of delivery, it makes Henrik beam. He jumps up to hug me loosely and takes his dishes to the sink. He continues out of the room, thumping up the stairs, to his room.

"Well played," Grant whispers and it brings a smile to my face. I love being a partner with him. Why can't he see past my idiosyncrasies to my value? He gazes at me with love but I'm more than a portrait. I'm still savoring his remark when he gives me a chaste kiss on my forehead as he leaves the table. The action is a major step forward for our fragile truce. I'm left alone in the kitchen with my mouth hanging open.

Chapter 4

Munchkins.

The room looks to be painted by munchkins. At least the baseboards have been taped and paint speckled drop cloths protect the floors. Dark brown paint covers the bottom of the walls with strokes extending to my shoulder height like someone decided to decorate with giant mutant handprints.

"You may want to change out of your suit before we paint, Grant," says a feminine voice behind me.

I turn to see a very paint-splattered Alison. Her hair is hanging in two short pigtails under her ears. One of them is tipped with paint as if she had been using it to paint the walls instead of a brush. The light freckles over her nose are crowded by larger dots of paint. She looks nineteen years old again. She is wearing a small white shirt and shorts which reveal long paint-speckled limbs. A blob of paint is perched over her left breast, reminding me of chocolate sauce and the games to be played with it.

"What are you smirking about?" She asks, raising a graceful eyebrow. The delicate brown arch disappears in a cloud of red hair on her forehead.

"Munchkins," I reply. I silently thank the heavens for a quick retort having nothing to do with gravity-defying paint blobs.

Her eyes flick to the wall, then back at me. A slow

smile creeps across her face, followed by a quiet laugh. I laugh too; not because I think I'm hilarious but because I'm nervous about being alone with her. The intimacy between us has faded away over the years and it is just easier if we are never alone. We are busy people. Busy people are successful people.

After a quick clothing change, I find myself atop a ladder painting the highest point in Henrik's room. A Blink-182 song fills the room from Alison's phone along with her soft singing. She has climbed the bottom three ladder rungs to blend my efforts with the painting they had finished earlier. The position puts us so close I can smell her unique scent—garden and citrus. It also puts the top of her head at the level of my waist.

Oh Lord. She is slightly swaying toward the wall with each brushstroke. From where I am standing, she could be just as easily stroking something else entirely. I must hold my breath when she looks up to me, a small smile pulling on her lips.

"I think it's time to move the ladder," she says but I'm too stuck in my own fantasy for it to register. I watch her step off the ladder, bend down to put down her brush in the paint tray and reach for my mine. Her clothes do nothing to hide her curves and I'm delighted with the view of her stooped over the paint tray. I stand there staring, panting, waiting.

"Having you up there reminds me of the night we met," she says while dropping my brush in the tray, bending over again. "Remember? You had climbed up to prune the Minneola trees in the university greenhouse. You dropped your clippers into my astragalus hybrids."

"Yeah, wow," I say with a laugh as I move the

ladder to its new position, "were you angry."

"Only after you fell off your perch and squashed my plants," she laughs.

"Yes, but I got to squish you too," I retort, earning myself one of her biggest smiles. "I never did thank you for getting me through ecology. That grade was more yours than mine. I would have never survived."

"We spent so many hours studying. You earned that grade."

"YOU spent so many hours studying it. I was studying you more than books."

"Right. You were slick, even back then. Remember how you conned me into dinner the first night as a penance for ruining my semester project? We walked to a pizza place and got carry-out."

"I thought it was genius to get more time with you if I do say so myself."

"We ate pizza under the stars..."

"Until my fraternity brothers surprised us with water balloons. I could have killed them."

"I thought you were going to. The way you jumped up and chased them all the way back to the fraternity house."

"It wasn't all me. I remember you chasing them too. You always were a firecracker. I could tell from the moment we met."

"That's what you thought of me?"

"Yeah, I was looking for a firecracker, so I knew I had to spend more time with you," I say, climbing the ladder once more. We begin to work in silence for a while. The only sounds are the sounds of our brushes slapping the wall and the music playing softly from Alison's phone.

Two more walls are painted before I begin to feel drowsy. I have been on the go for more than twelve hours trying to balance my giant deadline at work and keeping my family happy. My brush begins to droop in my hand but I'm too slow to stop it. Drip! Two drops of paint fall right onto the top of Alison's head. Her head snaps up as she dismounts the ladder. I step down too in preparation for the tirade she will undoubtedly unleash upon me.

Splat! I feel a line of paint spray from my chin to my hairline. Startled, I open my eyes to find Alison giggling. It echoes around the room like tiny bells on a sleigh. I wait for the sound to die before making my next move. Catching her off guard, I fling paint across her shirt from one breast to the other.

Her jaw drops in shock and she looks down at my handiwork. I'm playing with fire now. It is exhilarating to watch her contemplate how to punish me. It doesn't even register when she flings paint across my shirt to match her own. We look like members of the same team, complete with matching jerseys. She turns to run deeper into the room, and I can't resist. I slap my paintbrush across her ass as she flees past me.

Instantly, she changes direction, charging at me. I catch her wrists and I easily remove her brush from her hand. I deposit both brushes into the paint tray. Holding her wrists between us, I study her face. It is flushed with her lips slightly parted. She's looking at my lips too. I lean in to gently brush a kiss over her lips. My blood instantly boils to a raging inferno. My body begins to make demands for more.

"Truce?" she asks quietly.

"Yes," I whisper back. Instantly she breaks the

spell, pulling from my arms. I'm left standing, wishing I could pull her back. I look up at the walls. We are nearly done.

"It's late and there's so little left. I can finish it," I say as I lean to retrieve my brush.

"How about I spot you from the bottom of the ladder?" she offers as I climb back up.

"Sounds good," I say and start painting. I listen to three more songs on her phone as I finish the painting. I climb down to find my safety net asleep at the bottom of the ladder. She's curled on her side, arms folded beneath her head. I watch her chest rise and fall with each breath. Long lashes rest on her cheeks and a small smile plays on her lips. My lips tingle with the memory of the small kiss we shared. An act so innocent has thrown me off balance.

I'm at a loss as to what to do. My body demands I wake her to at least get an explanation for her breaking our embrace or at most to get more action. My heart wishes to carry her to our new bed, tuck her in, and hold on to this playful version of her. My brain says to leave her sleeping. Stepping over her boundaries and touching her without invitation could ruin all our work to get along. We haven't had a huge screaming match since we moved. Having a peaceful household has been vital to me. I must be at the top of my game to become an asset at Bergan. If they have enough new products we could settle here while living like royalty, but what good is a lonely throne?

Chapter 5

"And then he left me sleeping on the floor!" I exclaim while throwing my arms in the air. I am sitting with Rosie Paulino in her deserted restaurant dining room on Monday afternoon. Under the guise of getting our sons to socialize, we have a standing coffee date.

"No," Rosie replies with eyes wide as saucers.

"Oh yes. I woke up sticking to the drop cloth, the lights off and no husband in sight. What do you think it means?"

"That he's a walking dead man. What did he say on Sunday?"

"He said nothing. He vanished until dinner time and by then, I was over it."

"Were you really over it?"

"No, but it felt silly to ask about the previous night when he was away all day. I couldn't even ask where he had been. I get so tongue-tied around him. I thought if I let it all go, I could have more of the fun we had on Saturday—before he ditched me that is. How did you handle this stuff with Frankie?" I lament.

"We didn't dance around each other. We danced with each other. I'm sad he's gone but we savored every drop of time that life gave us. You are so busy worrying about being good enough for Grant you are being less than you. You two must learn how to talk to each other which means you, Alison, need to open up. I was never afraid of what Frankie would say because I knew we would talk until the silly matter was resolved. Frankie was that kind of guy. I knew it from our wedding day to the day he died," she says.

"Oh Rosie, I'm sorry if you don't want to talk about him," I say when her eyes start to glaze with unshed tears.

"I'm remembering our wedding day," she pauses to blow her nose on her napkin and then asks, "don't you ever sit and think about your wedding day?"

"There is not much to think about because I was already pregnant with Henrik. A wedding came about because Grant and I were arguing on whose last name Henrik would have. Grant decided it would become a non-issue if we married. I was so smitten with him I wanted to marry too. So off to the courthouse we went with my parents. They were thrilled he was so honorable; he was marrying me without their intervention.

"After that, we still lived separately with our respective parents. Grant finished his degree in record speed and started climbing the corporate ladder. I moved in with him after Henrik had started school and then I got a job teaching a few gardening classes at the local nursery," I say.

"My word woman, you have a story much sadder than mine! I'm supposed to be the sob story! A poor widow with too many kids!" Rosie wails as she flings a hand over her face with a flourish.

"Oh no, I don't mean for it to sound like that," I say within my laughter, "I'm more at home in the dirt than a big white dress. Could you really imagine me head-to-toe in lacy bows? Not happening. Besides, my mother always said it is supposed to be more about the man than the day."

"You mean the one who left you sleeping on the floor," she retorts.

I let out a big unfeminine laugh. "Yes, that's the one. What am I going to do?"

"Eat some tortellini," calls Henrik. He comes through the kitchen doors carrying plates of tortellini salad followed by Rosie's three younger sons.

"Did you make all the tortellini before stopping to make lunch?" Rosie asks with narrowed eyes.

"Yes Mom," says Tommy, her youngest. "You should have seen Henrik's fingers fly. He's a pasta folding machine!"

"Piano fingers," Henrik says with modesty. He flexes his fingers for emphasis.

"Yeah Mom, Henrik did more than half the dough all by himself. We used three pounds to make the salad, froze two pounds to make the fried appetizer and now we will wrap up the final six pounds in the cooler for entrees," says Anthony, her fifth son.

"Well, thank you for serving us, boys. I'm so glad Henrik is learning these skills from you," I say. All the boys beam with pride and my heart fills to see them getting along so well. Henrik has befriended all the Paulino boys much more closely than any of the friends he had at school in Ohio. Gone is the angry boy who was getting in fights with every adult in his path. That boy has been replaced with a champion pasta folder with a passion for music and a crew of multi-aged friends.

"It's the least they can do after you gave them a botany lesson this morning. I really appreciate that you agreed to take over teaching math and science. Science was Frankie's forte, not mine," Rosie says, inspecting her tortellini with her fork.

"We will see if they learned anything by how long they keep their oregano seedlings alive," I retort, pointing my fork at each boy.

With that, Rosie addresses the boys again, "Okay troops, what do you need to do next?"

"Make pizza dough, divide it, weigh it and wrap it," Anthony replies with a mock salute.

"Well hop to it! Then use the extra dough to make lunch for yourselves," Rosie commands.

Crash! We are all startled by loud noises coming from the kitchen. We sit in silence waiting for Rosie to decide what to do next. "Don't worry, I'm okay," calls a voice from the other side of the door.

"Ray, I'm counting on you in there," Rosie calls back. Not wanting to be part of the crossfire, the younger boys take this opportunity to run back into the kitchen. The swinging door is the only evidence of their arrival in the dining room.

"Do you think Ray and Frank Junior are feeling cheated being in the back with the younger boys while we are in here?" I ask.

"Ray is happy to be somewhere he doesn't have to be the center of attention. He's so quiet. It's getting better with him now waiting tables, but I can tell he hates the customer interaction. Junior is on the brink of burnout. He wants to be his father so much, but no one can do everything Frankie did every day. The man was a miracle," Rosie says becoming tearful again. I reach over and give her a hug. I feel so terrible she has lost Frankie. The love between them must have been so powerful. I wish I could have seen them together. It makes me feel guilty for wasting so many years estranged from Grant.

"Is there anything I can do to help? You or the kids?" I ask when we part the embrace.

"For me? I have a battery-operated boyfriend to help me out, but thanks for offering," Rosie says, sniffling with laughter. I turn red which only makes her laugh harder.

"I meant the burdens of the restaurant, crazy woman," I say laughing too.

"I need to reduce the amount of time people are waiting to get in. No one will want to stand outside when winter comes with snow and frigid temperatures. Frankie would go along the line and handle carry out orders to sort those people out of line. However, we physically do not have an extra body to walk up and down the entrance."

"What if you rearranged the entrance to divide the line into two parts: Dine in and Carryout? If people sorted themselves then you wouldn't need an extra person. Look at Anthony's leadership skills, down there. At eleven years old, he looks ready to lead a kitchen brigade. That would free up Vinnie and you to help Ray with the small talk in the dining room. Frank Junior could answer the phone while he runs the register, right?"

I watch her eyes light up and a smile spread across her face. Her entire posture changes as I speak. I see hope blooming inside her and I wish I had inquired about her troubles earlier.

"You are the best! I couldn't see the solution through the everyday grind. Let's draw this up for the boys…" Rosie trails off as she observes my sorting of my plate contents. She raises the edge of her dark brows and frowns at me. Oh no, I forgot she had never seen me eat. I feel I owe her an explanation especially since we are growing so close. I take a centering breath, blink heavily and put my fork down. "I have a condition. I have sensory processing disorder," I blurt out.

"I have never heard of that. What does it mean exactly?" Rosie asks.

Feeling encouraged by the compassionate look on her face, I continue. "It means some of my senses are heightened and some are dampened. Which senses fall into which categories is different for each person with the disorder. It's genetic, so Henrik's musical ear is an extension of my heightened hearing. I can hear fluorescent lights buzzing, footsteps approach me before anyone else does and everyone's conversations around me.

"Therefore, I avoid crowds including your restaurant when it's open. I need to separate my food by texture too. Crunchy foods can scratch the inside of my mouth if I don't chew it aggressively. I feel soft foods squish on my teeth. Flavors and scents are also more intense for me as well. I'm really great at guessing at what is in dishes because each ingredient stands out so much, even just by smell."

"Well, at least there's a name for your weirdness. Did you get a hard time about it when you were a kid?" she asks, waving a tortellini pillow on her fork at me.

"There was a lot of weirdness for kids to needle when I was in school. I come from a long line of odd women. My mother has full conversations with the moon and claims he sends her signs to guide her. I have aunts who read tarot cards, runes and crystals. My grandmother was an herbal healer. She was the one who first taught me about plants and inspired my career choice.

"Kids aren't accepting so I avoided situations where they could be introduced to my family. Honestly, I was kind of relieved when Henrik agreed to be homeschooled and focus on his music. It would have been a much easier childhood for me if that had been an option," I say, shuffling the tomatoes to their own side of my plate.

"I couldn't see sending my hoard an hour away to school each day either," Rosie agrees. "My Frankie grew up homeschooling in this restaurant with his siblings as free labor for his mom. Gran would throw a fit if I sent the boys away."

"I really appreciate the boys' inclusion of Henrik. He seems to fit right in. I was worried about having access to friends," I say earnestly.

"The boys are happy for another pair of hands. I also appreciate him playing piano on Saturday nights. No one has touched it since Gran quit playing," Rosie says indicating the old upright piano in the corner with her fork.

"Everything is falling into their place here…"

"Except you. I can hear in your voice that you need more. You need to make a move on Grant. Haven't you ever pursued him?"

"Never," I say examining a speckle of pepper, "in the beginning, we didn't need any encouragement. Then when we reunited, we were too busy fighting to be romantic. We even had separate bedrooms for the last four years. It's hard to put myself out there when don't even feel comfortable being alone with him."

"That's why you were left on the floor. You need to act all-in if you tell him you are all-in. You said he doesn't listen to you. He can't read your mind, so you need to give him signals. Even Frankie needed signals and we were tuned to the same frequency. Grant's just a man, not a supernatural figure," Rosie says pointing her index finger at me.

"When we moved here, we moved into the same room," I start until I take in Rosie's glare. "Okay, Love Guru, teach me your ways."

"Now we are talking," she says rubbing her hands together. "First, we need to rinse off some of that dirt and find out what color your skin really is, Pig-Pen."

"Haha, very funny," I say with another eye roll.

"Seriously, and you need something lacy. Maybe something red to complement your hair color? Then you need to fill your bedroom with flowers and candlelight…"

"Cheesy much? I don't think I could pull it off."

"If you want magic then you need to be blatant in your intentions. He's probably scared to death to get too close. No one wants rejection from their spouse. If Frankie would have pushed me away, even not holding my hand, I would have felt crushed. No this is serious, like rose petals on the floor, serious," Rosie says grabbing my phone off the table.

"I don't think I can do this…"

"Awesome. Red, lacy and same-day delivery!" Rosie says to my phone.

"What?!" I squeak.

"Rosie, to the rescue. You have everything else at

ɔ seduce him. How about Friday when he's not
.ing of work?" Rosie says showing me the
ɔhase receipt on my phone screen. I put my face into
ɑy hands and groan. I can't believe I'm going to
attempt this when it is so far out of my comfort zone.
What will Grant say?

"He always orders from Paulino's on Fridays.
When he calls in the order, I will send Ray over to pick
up Henrik for a sleepover with my boys. Then you can
get him, Girl! I'll put together a meal you can feed each
other like those cartoon dogs who share the spaghetti,
only you better be the tramp! I don't think he has it in
him," Rosie suggests. She looks so excited while I feel
nauseous with anxiety.

Am I really considering this? Just the thought of
propositioning Grant makes my heart skip a beat. I feel
so self-conscious around him. All he sees is a burden,
will a piece of red lace be enough for him to see me as a
woman again? I finally manage to push a grumbling
reply through my lips, "thanks, I will. I'm a romantic at
heart. I can't have a marriage of convenience anymore.
I need the courage and for Grant to spend some time at
home."

"Spending some time in bed instead of sleeping on
the floor would be an upgrade too!" Rosie says
laughing. I throw my napkin at her as I join in laughing.

Chapter 6

"You moved a truckload of data over the last two days. What did you do? Spend the weekend here?" asks James.

The IT specialists are hanging out in my office again. I almost wish someone would fry the mainframe so I can get some more work done. I have my task lists from Saturday and Sunday staring at me with only half the items crossed off. I need to get moving but my mind can't stay focused. I start consolidating my task lists into a master task list. That's what I need: a nice organized list. "Is that what your job is—to spy using the company network?"

"Pretty much. We feel the pulse of the company. We know who is emailing whom and when. We keep a list. When Santa brings his bonus checks, he sees us first," Nate replies.

"Well, elves, hold on to your pointy shoes. I have got Azolicyst going out of the door today," I announce.

"What?!" my colleagues squeak simultaneously.

"Yes, I sent the email to Brad this morning. I finished my group's labeling work over the weekend. Gone are the days of paginating binders, thank goodness. It's all electronic so I uploaded it into the gateway early this morning. Didn't you see that in your spying?" I ask.

"I came in to congratulate you but seeing the smirk

on your face tells me your ego is inflated enough," says a voice from my doorway. It is Brad, the CEO, and owner of Bergan. Everyone freezes as he waltzes over to my side of the desk. He claps a hand on Nate's and James's shoulders as he passes them as if he is marking his territory.

"Thanks, but it was really a team effort. Hopefully, this is just the first submission in a long line. Getting this out will give us ten months of breathing room while the FDA reviews it. I'm hoping to get Julibamar submitted during the interim. That reminds me, I must contact the labs and see when they started stability testing. Stability testing must be a year in at the time of submission, so they really run our timeline," I babble while still scribbling my lists together.

Brad laughs. "He's already on to the next one. I haven't even spread the good news around the company and he's on to the next one! Good Lord! Slow down, kid. You will burn out at this pace."

"You hired me to accelerate patient solutions. The best way is to layer your products so there is a constant stream of FDA communications. I have to get the snowball rolling to create the avalanche," I reply.

Brad claps his hand on my shoulder. "Celebrate the big win. You have made a big impact on the team. Come by my office later. I want to talk about long term incentives. You are a leader I want to keep."

"Oh, thank you. Yes, I will come by this afternoon. I have some ideas about a Saccharomyces boulardii generic. Could I run them by you then?" I stammer with a wide grin. Nate and James are exchanging covert looks. *Great*. They are probably going to toilet paper my office when I go home.

Brad laughs again. "A third project? You are just what I have been looking for. Someone to drive us."

Who is he addressing? He says this when he isn't looking at me. He is looking at Nate and James. What do the two IT specialists have to do with the direction of the company? They are specialist level, not even middle management. I have a prickly feeling I am missing something. Hopefully, when I have time with Brad alone later, I will feel more positive. After all, he is offering more money. If only money could buy happiness.

Chapter 7

The best part of being a busy person is that hours fly by and it seems to always be the weekend. Developing a routine and checking items off my lists helps my mood too. I got the green light from Brad to start an ANDA—Annotated New Drug Abbreviated— on our first generic. It is such a simple way to bring extra money to the company. I was surprised Brad had never heard of one. Scientists who develop drugs cost money in the beginning not make money. Hopefully, the money from the generic would help the company fund their work and their households.

I met with chemists to start identifying the market drug's formulation to copy and to get an estimated timeline on stability testing. The best part of making a generic is the copying company can use the original company's clinical trials and long-term stability data. We only need six months of stability data, so it won't take a miracle to have the generic into the FDA pipeline before the review of Azolicyst is complete. Add Julibamar, our new Schizophrenia biologic, to the mix and the employees of Bergan have job security. That is a huge victory for small-town Kentucky.

On a roll, I call Rosie to place my weekly carry-out order. I check my phone that I had dialed the correct number when a decidedly masculine voice answers. "Uh, hi", I stammer. I am caught off guard but recover enough to add: "I need a carry-out order for Grant Luther."

"Yeah, hey, it's Frank. Mom has it ready, so I'll fire it now."

"But I haven't given you my order…" I start.

"Mom put something together this afternoon. Do you want to tell her to do something else? I'll put her on the phone and let you tell her."

"No, no. I'm sure she knows best," I reply, noticing how he doesn't volunteer to pass the message himself. Smart men don't question Rosie Paulino, especially the ones raised by her.

"Good choice. See ya in a bit," Frank replies and abruptly hangs up the phone.

Check. Check. Check. It feels so good to have a completed task list. Happy Friday to me. I gaze around my office with satisfaction, stretching my back to give it relief from being hunched over my laptop for so long. I stare at the soft albeit very ugly yellow couch in my office under a giant whiteboard. I don't think anyone has ever sat on that monstrosity.

I walk to my left to clean the whiteboard, covered with multicolored strategies and musing from the frequent visitors to my office. I had transferred those thoughts to tasks, documents, and correspondence during the week's work. It feels cathartic to put them to rest. I strut past the door to throw away my cleaning wipes and stare at my empty bookshelves. I keep my office without personal effects, knickknacks or clutter to focus on the task at hand.

One of my secrets to success is my unwavering focus on the company's goals. Alison knows not to call, visit, or otherwise interrupt my workday unless it is an absolute emergency. I swagger back to my sparse desk and line up my pens, blotter, laptop dock and notepads with precision. The top page of my notepad contains my weekend task list, so I rip it off and fold it neatly into my pocket before leaving for the weekend.

As I open Bergan's front door, I am welcomed by a blast of cold air. Winter is fast approaching, and the leaves are running from their branches. Only the Poplar trees still hold onto their golden treasure like disgruntled pirates. The ground is soggy, muddy and I am thankful for my wider sport grade tires. Without them, my car would likely slide off the road and into a leaf-covered sink-hole. I am also thankful for my heated seats as I start the car.

The line is trailing onto the sidewalk outside of Paulino's as I approach. I take my spot in the queue and try to peek through the windows at the happy diners inside without being obtrusive. I am a few minutes later than usual. Through the blinds, Nate and James are moving to a table, so I have no one to harass to pass the time in line. Luckily for me, the line moves much faster than usual. When I arrive at the counter, I can see how this feat is accomplished.

The phone has been moved to the other side of the ancient register and Frank Junior is stationed in front of it with a sign over his head that reads "carry out only". I watch him answer the phone, write the ticket, and then call out orders to the kitchen brigade between customer transactions.

Anthony is gathering order parts as customers give him their names at the carry out station while assisting Tommy at the pizza ovens. Rosie stands at the side seating diners who want to eat within the restaurant, refilling drinks in the dining room, while keeping a close eye on her boys. The atrium now moves like a machine, mirroring the efficiency of the kitchen.

"This is incredible," I tell Rosie as I approach.

"It was the suggestion of your wife. She has a talent for leading the troops. She said it was from when she taught big classes, but I think she's a natural," Rosie says with a waggle of her brow.

"Really? She suggested this?" I counter.

"Tell her that I thank her, it's working, and she needs to find a way to come in to watch Henrik tomorrow," Rosie replies, counting the items on her fingers.

"I don't know about that. It's easier to keep her in our home. She couldn't handle this level of activity."

"I bet she could. On Saturday night, we turn on the table lights, and everyone is quieter to listen to Henrik play. Suggest it. Better yet, tell her I suggest it."

Not wanting to argue, I nod and turn to Frank. I'm used to having to make excuses for Alison to stay out of busy events. I pay and receive a bag of smaller bags. "No pizza boxes?" I ask before I can censure myself.

"It's pizza deconstructed. Why put it together when Alison will just take it apart?" Anthony asks with a shrug.

I have to admit the kid has a point. My only concern is how he knows about Alison. Surely, she is keeping her strange eating habits from her new friends to fit in. Maybe asking Alison about the time she spends at Paulino's during the day will prove to be a way to break the ice.

I pull out my weekend task list and jot it down. Lifting my bags, I thank Anthony and set back out to my car. When I get to my parking space, I hear the roar of motorcycles. Nate and James are speeding away. Why would they leave a coveted Paulino's table without eating?

My mind whirls in chaos as I hope there isn't trouble at Bergan. Disastrous possibilities going on at Bergan plague my thoughts as I drive home. I drive as fast as I dare through the drizzly conditions. I check my email using the car's system. I have no messages. Trees blur past as I rush home. I use voice-to-text to message Nate and then James to get a status update on the network.

When I get no response, I contemplate turning around and heading back to work. I decide to stay my course when fog settles over the road ahead of me. I am almost home where I could check the network on my laptop. I pass a few farms and soon I will be at our property. I manage to turn on my high beams even though I am driving as if on autopilot.

"Holy shit!" I yell into the darkness. I wretch my wheel to the left and barely miss a big white blur. Was that a giant cat, cow, or a small horse? I don't have time to ponder what has crossed my path. I am too busy juggling the wheel like a driver in a 1960s spy movie. My car skips off the road to go for an adventure in the fields.

Long grass becomes cornstalks which become large trees. My car ricochets like a pinball off each tree with a crunching sound. One headlight is knocked out and then the second goes dark too. I can't see, can't steer and can't stop until an octogenarian oak tree does all three items for me. The last thing I see is my airbag deploying.

Chapter 8

When the red and white striped pickup truck pulls up the drive, I laugh so hard I feel tears in my eyes. I'm not sure whether it's my nerves at tonight's events or the giant white wolf-head perched on top of the truck's cab that causes my fit of giggles. I have never seen the Paulino's parade vehicle before tonight. I guess it is Ray's vehicle since Frank got the first choice and wisely chose the van.

"Henrik, Ray's here," I call upstairs from the atrium. I hear thumping across the second floor and down the stairs as he approaches. I'm so nervous for him. He's never spent a night away from me. However, he was ecstatic when I asked him about it a few days ago. My little boy is growing up.

"Love ya, Mom," Henrik says trying to run past me out the front door.

"Wait a minute, Mister. Did you pack pajamas? What about your evening medicines? Do you want to grab your pillow, so you sleep more comfortably?" I fire at him. He stops and stares wild-eyed at me.

"Take my pillow? Really, Mom? The guys will never live that down! I have pjs, evening medicines, and my toothbrush. I'm fine," he says raising his hands in the air.

"I just worry. It's what moms do," I say, trying to pull him into a hug. I get to kiss his head before he shakes me off. He runs his fingers through his hair in a gesture that reminds me of Grant. We both turn to the door as a car horn sounds on the other side. I'm reminded of the urgency of getting Henrik away before Grant heads home.

"I have clothes and my piano books for tomorrow night's service at the pizzeria too. I'm good," he says walking out of the door.

"Love you too, Sweet Boy," I say closing the door behind him. I take a deep centering breath and close my eyes. I need to organize my thoughts and reduce my anxiety. I take off my proverbial mom-hat as my thoughts switch from Henrik to Grant.

I walk to the kitchen balcony where I retrieve some small pots of dirt and tulip bulbs I had stashed there during the week. Taking them up to the bedroom, I also grab the Amazon packages Rosie had ordered in my name. Now the stack is higher than my head and I'm stumbling over each stair. *What am I doing?* I finally reach the bedroom and gingerly set down my bounty. Unwrapping the packages, I tackle the atmosphere first.

Our green bedroom is dominated by a large four-poster bed. It is so tall the top of the mattress is parallel with my ribcage. There is barely enough room left for the bedside tables, dressers, and full-length mirror.

I place a pot with a single bulb on each surface. Sticking my fingers in the dirt with the bulb, causes the bulb to grow into a small plant. I hold the top of the plant in my other hand and it softly blooms into a dark red cup. I place a candle in front of the pot and repeat these steps on every surface. When the room is set, I stop in front of our full-length mirror. I giggle as I take in my mud-splattered appearance. It will take a miracle to transform me into a seductress. I feel a sense of urgency when a shaft of pink light peeks through the blinds from the setting sun. Grant will be home very soon.

After a quick shower, shave, and several handfuls of shampoo, I am finally clean. I paint my nails red with the polish in the delivered package, ever thankful that Rosie has thought of everything I would miss.

Only one item left and it's still sitting inside the crinkly plastic at the bottom of the box. With a sigh and a look over my shoulders, I take the scrap of lace out of the package. *Isn't there another piece to this?* than it looked in the online ad with not much material involved.

I decide to take a chance and slip it on. I frown at myself in the mirror. At least I do not have a farmer's tan as I tend to freckle in the sun due to my Irish heritage. The lingerie covers all the necessary bits, but barely. I only wish it covered the marks from being pregnant all those years ago. I'm so nervous imagining all the different outcomes when Grant comes home. Standing in front of the mirror criticizing myself isn't helping, so I start lighting candles.

When I turn off the overhead lights, I have to laugh at the absurdity of being surrounded by small fires. This bedroom scene looks more likely out of Dante's Inferno than a romance novel. I have visions of my house burning down and having to explain to the Strawberry Fire Brigade why I had so many candles lit at the same time. I separate the pots from the candles a little more to satisfy my neurosis.

My last effort is to pull out the bag of flower petals I salvaged from pruning the flowers in the landscaping.

I couldn't bring myself to sacrifice one rose to spread flower petals over the room, so I gathered a couple of outer loose petals from each of our flowers. This way no flowers had to suffer from being removed, just a late pruning.

With a path of petals leading into the room and around to his side of the bed, I'm at a loss as to what to do with myself. I curl up on the bed with a book to stare at while I wait for him. Hopefully, he's home soon so my heart will stop pounding.

Chapter 9

"What the hell Nate? You know how pissed Brad will be if we just killed Grant?" I hear a masculine voice yell. I am drifting in and out of consciousness, stuck in a weird dream version of the accident aftermath.

"This plan always works. Who knew he drove that fast?" replies a second voice.

"Have you ever heard him talk about his car? Oh 258-foot pounds of torque, oh 335 horsepower, oh, oh, oh," the first voice says, mocking my speech pattern.

"Well, you always say how much you hate the blood draining part. There's more of his blood inside the car than inside his body," the second voice quips.

"Why don't you wash up, while I get this done?" I place the first voice as my co-worker, James. His blurry form seems to be slashing his wrist with a pocketknife. Drops of James's blood drips into my mouth and my stomach threatens to heave it back at him. I drift out of consciousness and my battered body starts convulsing almost immediately.

"We've got a live one, Sargent," the second voice says. It must be Nate warning James as they are never apart. James rolls me onto my side. The movement brings me to a semi-conscious state. Distantly I hear my car turn off following James calling Josh's Gas and Auto for a tow truck. The last thing I hear before passing out again is James saying he is sending a text to Brad to report that the deed is done.

"My car!" I groan as I become conscious again. The world is on its side as the grass under my face lays on the left side of my field of vision. It is a relief to move my eyes without becoming dizzy. I can clearly see my car propped on its side against a giant tree. The driver's door is open but standing straight up like a flag of surrender. The axles are broken, positioning the wheels at odd angles. There are so many various fluids leaking from the car that I decide not to examine closely as the whole area has a faint smell of gasoline.

A smear of brown fluid connects me to the wreckage site like an umbilical cord. Bits of glass litter the ground like snow and I can feel it like a coating all over my body. Surprisingly, I don't feel pain just total exhaustion as if I beat up my car with my fists and won.

"Look, James, our patient is waking," Nate jokes when I struggle to lift my head.

"Aaaaaahhhhhh!" I yell hysterically. Propped against the back of my thighs is a giant talking and now laughing cat. I can't help my panic at being in such proximity to such a dangerous animal. I try to jump to my feet but only my head moves. The rest of the world, however, starts spinning around, even the cat.

"Wow, Brad's prediction that he would turn quickly was spot on," says the talking cat. It is white with black spots, causing me to guess it is a snow leopard of some sort. It stretches its front paw and licks between each claw. Then it bends its head to bite at them all the while keeping its gaze focused on me.

I stare at the cat with wide eyes. How does a cat know my boss? I must have a concussion. Maybe I'm dead. Do dead people hallucinate? I wiggle my fingers and sniff the wet grass beneath me. Too many of my senses are working for me to be dead. I am probably in a drug-induced coma somewhere. Alison is probably bawling at my side while machines beep and whir as background music. Only one way to test this. I place an image of a scantily dressed Alison firmly in my brain and...

"Yep, he's coming out of it. Good thing too. Carrying him back to his house would be a bitch," James says as he pops into my view.

Ugh, not a dream. Not a hallucination. I am lying in a field, completely helpless, probably paralyzed for life and my rescue is Laurel and Hardy A. K. A. the IT department of Bergan. I strain my eyes to look farther afield. I recognize the trees as being the ones to the west of my house but still on my property. I see the sun starting to rise and realize I never came home last night. The thought of my wife bawling at my side in a hospital looks much more attractive now.

She is going to explode when she sees me next. This will remind her of the stunts I used to pull in Ohio. She will assume I have been at some bar. My only hope is that I can bring James home with me, without my car, to explain what happened. Or maybe I need to bring the talking cat...I look over hoping he is a figment of my imagination...yep, he's still there.

"I love how every time he looks at me, he freaks out. Check this out! Roar!" The cat says while flashing his teeth but doesn't move from my back. I startle and he rolls around on the ground with laughter. The instinctive fear of giant cats is slowly being defeated by my rational side. If it was going to eat me, he would

51

have already started while I was passed out. Now that I can raise my head, I check my limbs. Since I have all fingers and toes accounted for, I am relieved to be in no physical danger from the cat. However, if my wife throws me out, I will have a bed in the nearest mental hospital.

"Nate stop it. I never know how to begin the talk. I need to think," James snaps at the cat.

"Nate? Did you call the cat Nate? Someone needs to start talking because details of my drive home are starting to come back as is the feeling in my limbs," I say in a crescendo as my temper starts to rise.

"Great starting point. Nate and I are shifters. We can shift into our power animals. So yeah, Nate is the talking cat, but he prefers to be called a leopard. Today is your unbirthday, Alice, because now you are a shifter too," James starts.

"You two are crazy."

"Brad's orders so you can stop giving us the stink eye," says Nate the cat.

"I must be dreaming but too concussed to control my own dream," I interrupt. "Ouch!" I then yell when Nate nips at my arm. I stare wide-eyed at him. Did he just grin at me? Blue eyes are crinkled above the cat's long snout. The snout must be longer than a typical snow leopard's snout to accommodate Nate's big human nose. How am I even trying to rationalize my co-worker is in a cat body?

James snaps his fingers in front of my face. "You are a sharp guy, so stay with me. Our town is full of shifters who are at war with the Fae. They have even brought a fortress from their realm to sit just outside of town, which houses their exiled criminals called,

Sluagh. Brad picked you for our army because he sees your organizational skills, aggressive ambition, and less-than-sparkly personality."

"Fae, shifters, Sluagh," I say inching away from them. "You wrecked my car because you are mythical creatures who need my help in fighting more mythical creatures. Insanity."

"As soon as we know what animal you have been dealt, you can hopefully be a fighter for us. Brad really wants us to watch you because he suspects you are our next leader. We lost our previous leader in the last battle, so we are unorganized which leaves an opening for the Fae," James explains.

"What do you mean what animal? I can't turn into an animal, are you nuts? That's impossible," I stammer.

"Hello, remember me, talking snow leopard," Nate interjects.

"Oh, you are going to be a pain in all this," James says, raking a hand through his dark hair. The action makes it stand up in all directions. "Hold on to your task lists. We staged your accident to drain your blood. I performed a makeshift blood transfusion with my blood that's laced with a parasite."

"You gave me a parasite? I think I'm going to hurl."

"The parasite in your system is working on your DNA. It exposes codes turned off by evolution. That's why you feel as if you have been run over by a bulldozer.

"The animal you most resemble will have the most dormant code in your DNA. When it's turned on by the parasite, *BAM*! You are the animal with your brain, personality and memory embedded in it. The DNA conversion will finish in a week at most, based on how far you have come already."

"I'm all the things Brad wants because I'm busy. I don't have a week for this. I've got priorities over Dr. Doolittle genetics and fairy hocus pocus," I complain.

"Look at it this way, now you will be even more valuable to Brad and Bergan. You may even end up as his boss if you are the leader of the pack. The pack owns Bergan and the strongest shifters are the board. To be chairman, you have to be a predatory animal with the ability to partial shift," James says.

"Wouldn't I turn into a snow leopard because Nate turned me?" I stammer.

"Actually, James turned you. I was a diversion for your car accident, remember?" Nate snickers.

"We agreed you had to be the diversion because you could guard us better in power form than I can," James snaps at Nate.

"So I will be the same animal as James. What are you? Werewolf? Lion?"

Ignoring my question, he says: "Grant, you have been passed out for hours and I had a little recovery time from turning you too. We are out in the middle of your yard and I doubt you swept for Sluagh recently."

"Nope, the Sluagh definitely weren't mentioned as maintenance when I bought the house, in the new employee orientation or as part of the job interview," I babble hysterically.

"You are going to feel terrible for a few days but gradually get more strength and bulk than you have ever had in your life. Your senses will be sharper. You will feel more powerful. Don't worry, you will love it. Moreover, Bergan Pharma is depending on you and we know you love Bergan Pharma," James explains.

"Is that what everyone thinks? What Brad thinks? I'm so married to my job that I would trade my humanity for it? Married…ugh…what will Alison say? We are supposed to be working on getting closer and now she's snuggling up to a zoo exhibit?" I groan.

"Slow your roll there, Chief," Nate starts. "Alison can't know about any of this. She can live in ignorant bliss. We don't intend on turning anyone who wouldn't be an asset in the war."

"No girls allowed. Are you crazy? Keeping something this large from my wife will be impossible. I will just have to turn her myself," I say while starting to stand up. I have a small celebration when I can get to my feet without the ground tipping.

"Not an option. There are only three ways to become a shifter. The first is to grow into an adult after being the offspring of at least one shifter, which she's not. The second is to have a blood exchange with a born shifter, which you aren't. The third is to be a witch who has sex with a shifter. Are you telling me you are freaked out over Nate's power form but suddenly have a witch as a wife?" James says.

"No, my wife is ordinary. Well not completely ordinary but she's not magical. No pointy hats or broom riding," I say.

"Good. If you can stand guard with me, Nate will shift, and we will head to your house. When you shift back to human form it zaps your energy, so he will be out of it for a bit. I have already called Josh and the tow truck will be here soon to deal with your car. You can change clothes and bike with us back to Bergan to finish your transformation," James instructs me like I'm an errant schoolboy.

"Go back to Bergan after being gone all night? How am I supposed to get that past Alison?" I ask incredulously.

"Figure it out while watching the skies. Trust me, the Sluagh are much more terrifying than a wife could ever be. Besides I've seen you cut trained professionals into ribbons with your words; you should be able to appease your wife with them," James says with his eyes scanning the sky. He pulls a pair of sai from the back pockets of his jeans. I recognize them from the ninja turtle cartoons I watched as a child. They look so natural in the hands of my coworker that I am momentarily stunned.

Nate begins to tense up. His paws shrink into hands and feet. His tail dissipates as his limbs and torso lengthen. The last to change is his fur to human skin. A totally human Nate is lying in the grass, convulsing, after just a few minutes. I stand with a shocked expression unable to take my eyes from the transformation.

"Do we need to do anything? Why is he shaking so much? Is he in pain?" I ask as soon as my lips can move.

"The answers are: No. It's normal. No. Anything else? Keep your eyes to the sky and be wary of cold drafts. We will teach you to shift as fast as Nate, how to recover from shifting, and how to control shifting when your temper is tried. Just not now," James snaps. He reaches for a backpack leaning against the car and pulls out clothes for Nate. As Nate gingerly sits up and dresses, James spins around and punches me in the jaw.

"What the hell?" I yell, spitting blood. If I lost a

tooth, I'm going to tear him to shreds. I pat gingerly at my mouth.

"Your clothes are covered in blood, but you have no wounds. Your new shifter status means you have super healing abilities. Do you want to explain that to your wife without mentioning said status? I didn't think so. Now you have been hit in the face by your airbag. You're welcome," James says, still scanning the sky.

"All ready. Let's move," Nate says wearily. We start walking across the yard toward the back of my house. I can't help but study Nate on the way. There are little traces of the talking cat I hadn't noticed before. While James and I step, Nate glides through the grass. Nate's blue eyes and distinctive nose were evident in the snow leopard form now that I see his human face again. His hands are large for his height. I estimate they are the same size as his feet. They remind me of the large paws he was cleaning earlier.

"You aren't allowed to look any closer without buying me dinner first," Nate gripes.

"Sorry, I was looking for evidence of the talking cat."

"Snow leopard," he retorts.

When we reached the back edge of the gardens, a feminine voice calls from behind a hoop house. "Well, look what the cat dragged in?"

Nate and James snicker. I roll my eyes, losing hope they would help bail me out with my wife. After all, it is all their fault I am delayed.

She seems to appear out of nowhere, taking the air from my lungs. The only ray of sunshine on this gray morning finds its way through to spotlight her. Her shiny dark red hair oscillates under her chin like a fiery headdress. It matches the angry glow in her golden eyes, adding to her mystical appearance. She looks like the Celtic goddess Brigid, rising like a living flame to mingle with the common people. It takes all my strength to keep my jaw off the ground as she approaches.

"Lost your car again or just your phone so you couldn't call me? I was worried sick but now I see I had no reason to be worried," Alison fires at us. Her porcelain cheeks are flushed with her ire. My fingertips twitch as I resist the urge to stroke her face and absorb her heat. How is it I am always getting singed by her?

I know how this must look to her. Three exhausted men staggering up to the house at sunrise on a Saturday morning. Instead of alcohol, we smell like blood. She will believe her enhanced sense of smell even if she doesn't believe me.

"I was in a car accident. The BMW is totaled," I call back. As I approach her, I watch all the anger drain from her face. I'm sure she is taking in my bloody clothes, swelling jaw and split lip. I will have to remember to thank James next time we are alone.

"Are you okay? Where was the accident? Have you been to a hospital?" she says in a rush.

She runs her hands over me looking for injuries. I close my eyes and inhale her scent. It is intoxicating. I don't want to interrupt her exam in the hopes it will continue forever...or at least until I can get her alone. I shake my head to clear it. What is wrong with me? When I don't answer her, she stops her ministrations to look at me.

"He's got a little concussion. We were joyriding after a night at the bar and saw the accident aftermath.

He must have taken the turn too fast and slid into the ditch. The BMW was taken out by a tree. We got him out right away but waited until he came to before bringing him here," Nate says in my defense. I will have to bring the pair doughnuts on Monday in appreciation.

"But it didn't dawn on you to call an ambulance?" Alison demands, glaring at all of us. Even though she's a foot smaller than us, she points her chin with sass and defiance. Her fist is clenched against her hip which juts to the side. She looks magnificent even with dirt on her arms, hands, legs, and feet. It is as if she rose from the ground to light the Earth instead of the sun and lights up anyone in her path. On closer inspection, I realize she isn't wearing anything under that tiny tank. I must hold in a groan as she crosses her arms under her breasts lifting them slightly.

"I asked them to bring me home. You know how I hate being examined. I make a horrible patient," I say to call her attention to me. I watch her lashes fall as she closes her eyes. Her chest rises and falls as she takes a deep breath. I bite the inside of my cheek to keep my tongue in my mouth. What is wrong with me? My raging lust is making me act like a teenager. I look over to Nate and James who are glaring back at me.

A cold breeze blows over us. Nate and James immediately crouch into a fighter's stance gesturing toward the skies. Alison hugs herself tightly and shivers. Instinctively, I move closer to her. If this is the enemy, I am going to drop on top of her as a human shield. My body perks up at that. *Ugh*. Mortal danger and I'm getting broody. I hope this is a side effect of my near-death experience, not a new characteristic because I'm a shifter.

"Okay kids, we should get inside before someone catches a cold," James announces as the breeze fades. He is looking directly at me. Am I supposed to answer that?

"Henrik slept over at the Paulino's house last night. I can patch you up at least, but please shower in case he comes home. He will fear all that blood," she says to me.

Nate starts to pantomime something with his eyebrows as we walk into the house. I have no idea what he was trying to convey so I just say, "Thanks guys for bringing me back."

"Yes, thank you so much."

"If it's not too much trouble, could we get a cup of coffee before we travel back? We have been up all night too," James says in my direction. He is doing the same odd eyebrow gymnastics as Nate.

"Oh dear, I hadn't thought of that. Do you eat omelets? I have fresh dill from the garden this morning. It would be great in an omelet," Alison replies.

"That sounds like heaven," Nate drools.

I head for the shower while everyone else gets situated in the kitchen. Once I finish, and turn off the water, I can smell breakfast as clearly as if I am at the stove. I try to imagine myself as a giant cat or wolf running through the forest. I am surprised by how much I like the idea of being the apex predator, running free. This shifter thing is turning out to be cool, once I get past keeping things from Alison again. That sours my mood. There must be a way around that. I just have to find it.

"Knock, knock. Hey, I came to look at your

injuries," Alison says quietly as she steps through the door.

With all my daydreaming of being a star in a nature documentary, I haven't dressed as efficiently as I usually do. I am still naked with a towel casually slung over my shoulders when she enters. I watch her eyes bounce around, trying to find a safe place to look but always coming back to my groin. Her shyness makes me smile despite myself. I love how her face and neck are turning different shades of pink as she tries not to look at me. Like a good soldier, all of me stands at attention for her. I don't move, daring her to take this situation to a conclusion of her choice.

"I'm sorry. I guess I came up too quickly," she says to the floor.

My mind retorts she wasn't coming yet...

"My injuries are just to my face. I got punched, really hard...by the airbag. The rest of me is perfectly fine."

"You look perfect. I mean perfectly healthy. I mean mostly uninjured," she stammers. She places her tiny hand over her eyes.

Feeling braver than ever, I walk right up to her. I gently remove the hand from her face and hold it to my own. "See, I'm fine," I whisper as I gently rub my thumb over her tiny knuckles.

Her eyes lift to mine and lock our gazes. I have always found the golden color of her eyes fascinating but never studied them up close. They are light brown with a golden star in the middle. I am literally star‑gazing as she takes in the injuries to my face. We stand there for about a minute, lost in time.

I wonder if she is thinking about when we first

started dating, the hard times that followed, the present, or the future. I search her face for clues but don't want to break the spell by opening my mouth. I decide to put said mouth to better use by lowering my head toward hers.

Chapter 10

"Got a text from Brad. There's a problem with the submission. He wants all of us, at Bergan, now," James calls through the door as he pounds upon it.

"Sure, I'll be right down," Grant answers. He puts a finger to my lips to convey he wants me to stay quiet. I place a light kiss on his fingertip to push at his boundaries. His gaze meets mine and he takes a step forward to invade my space. *If James would go away…* Will Grant send his friends away?

"It sounds grim, Man," James continues.

I start to panic like a middle-schooler caught holding hands with a boy by her parents. I look to Grant to get us out of this embarrassing situation. He doesn't look alarmed in the slightest. I hope it means he has a plan.

"Gotcha," he says. So much for Grant saving the day; it looks like we are stuck here in the bathroom for eternity.

"And you need to pack a bag. This is a big…problem. It will take all weekend. You will be staying at the office most likely," James insists.

I make a silent wish that James isn't bold enough to open the door. I search my recollections frantically to remember if I locked it on the way in. I step back and look down at my feet. I can't do this with only half of Grant's attention and his coworker waiting at the door. I watch Grant pull the towel off his shoulders, secure it at his hips and leave the bathroom. He stomps over to his dresser in a fit of temper and tosses small stacks of clothes onto the bed.

He ransacks the closet and comes out with a duffle bag. Grant is giving packing heat a new meaning with the angry manner of his movements. He looks like he will explode. I stand stunned in the bathroom doorway as he slings the packed bag over his shoulder and starts to leave the room.

"You may want to put some of those clothes on your body, Boss," James says quietly.

Grant looks down at his waistline. He is heading to work in a towel. Grant gives James a scary look I have never seen before. James looks down at his feet and shuffles them. What, no come back? No emperor needs new clothes quip. The submission of the other man snaps Grant out of his red haze. Together the two men stomp downstairs leaving me alone in the bathroom. I can't believe both of them completely ignored me during their whole exchange. Maybe that was Grant's intention so I could avoid embarrassment. After all, he was the one seducing me when he had company.

"What was that?" I ask my reflection in the mirror. Grant's libido decides to wake after a decade of dormancy, now. Now, when he has guests in the kitchen, and we are nearly caught by one of them. If it is a side effect of the car accident, I hope it is permanent. Usually, Grant treats me in such a detached way. His honor code has kept him at a distance as if I am in such danger of breaking, even by his own hands. This morning he threw caution to the wind and approached me like a wife. I am stunned by his sudden change in personality.

My eyelashes flutter as I recall the encounter. I was frozen in place by the intensity of his blue eyes. They weren't their usual cold blue but scorching me to the bone like liquid nitrogen. I already miss the heat I could feel radiating from his body. My hand is still tingling from where he touched it, held it, and even caressed it. *Oh my...* I take a deep steadying breath which makes it worse. I am still standing in the steamy bathroom filled with his scent. I need to get a grip before he walks out the door.

As I race down the stairs, the three guys are lacing up their shoes in the front atrium. Grant has a duffle bag slung over his shoulder. I feel my heart rate accelerate. He can't leave now; not when we are getting along. We just had a breakthrough. We could talk...or...other stuff. "Must you go?" I hear myself ask. All three faces turn to the direction of my voice and I instantly feel a blush creep up my neck. I can't believe how pathetic I sound. It fits right into the dependent image Grant has of me.

"It's an emergency or we wouldn't pull him away. We would leave him here to recover," Nate answers.

"From the accident," James adds, looking at Nate.

"Does this mean you got Brad's text too?" I say to Grant.

His eyes grow wide, but it was Nate who again answers, "His phone must still be with the car."

"We will recover it from the tow company. Once Grant decides what to do with the car, he can get his personal stuff that was left behind," James adds.

I nod, losing the wind in my sails. He isn't my prisoner. I need to let him go if he is obliged to go. I rationalize Bergan keeps our family afloat but more importantly, it is what keeps Grant happy. Looking at the floor, I see his shoes step right against my toes. He catches my jaw in his hands to lift my chin. I only have time to inhale before his mouth crashes down on mine.

I only have time to inhale before his mouth comes down on mine. This action leaves my lips partially open and he takes full advantage. He tilts his head slightly to gain better access before plunging his tongue inside my mouth. His thumbs skim over my jaw as his fingers burrow into my hair. I instantly lean forward into his kiss and let myself surrender to him. My arms rise on their own accord to rest my hands on his shoulders.

His tongue tangles with mine before rubbing the insides of my cheeks, the roof of my mouth and around my teeth. This isn't a kiss goodbye for the weekend. This is a marking of territory. He claims every inch of my mouth as his own. As my confused brain fogs with lust, my heart soars.

When he lifts his head, we are both panting for air. He mumbles something about calling later which flies right by me. There is so much to say, so many emotions playing on his face, and I can't remember how to form words with my mouth. He turns and follows the other two guys out of our front door, closing it softly. I sit on the bottom stair to think. My brain is so scrambled all I can do is catch my breath.

Chapter 11

Hours later and in the garden, I'm still off-balance from Grant's bizarre behavior. Confusion, desire, and anger swirl around my aching head. Does Grant have a personality altering concussion or was it the fear of death that made him change? It certainly wasn't the surprise I had planned. He raced around the bedroom without noticing any of my preparations which were wilted from sitting out all night.

Crying had created a small pain between my eyes which was magnified this morning by my frustration with Grant. My distraction has sabotaged my gardening efforts too. Instead of clearing out the withered pumpkin vines, as I had planned, my unchecked magic has brought them back to life. Green vines adorn the raised bed where I have been working for the past half an hour...or has it been an hour?

A glance at my phone enlightens me to the two hours I have been sitting in the same spot. Paulino's will be opening in two more hours so I have enough time to consult my love guru. I hope she isn't as dumbfounded as I am over Grant's strange behavior.

"Hey Rosie, it's Alison. I need..." I start hesitantly when I hear the call connect.

"You are not saying that you aren't coming over. Ray and I will be in the dining room if you need support. I place you at the table by the piano too.

Having Henrik at your side will boost your confidence. Should I book you and Grant at 6 pm or 7 pm? You will want to eat and leave before eight because that's when the night staff at Bergan come in to eat together. It's a large, noisy group." Rosie projects over my voice.

"Wait. What?" I stammer.

"Grant didn't pass on the message that you are dining tonight when Henrik comes to play the piano? I bet you two were too busy to talk, right? Can't pass on messages with his mouth full? Giiiiiirl," Rosie snickers. I feel my face burning with embarrassment. I only wish she was right.

"Not quite but that's why I'm calling. I need you to be a love guru…" I start again.

"Hot Epsom salt bath with a little juniper berry in the bathwater. Following the bath, you need to chug cranberry juice for the rest of the day, as much as you can stand. This prevents a bladder infection as well as soothes bruising from, you know, when it got wild," she continues with no shame. I hope no one can hear this conversation. She may not get embarrassed but I'm turning into a cherry tomato at the thought of someone eavesdropping.

"No, Rosie, the only part of me bruised is my ego. Grant didn't come home until morning without calling," I start again.

"What? How is that possible? He left here on time. We didn't send Ray until Grant picked up your order," Rosie interrupts.

"He walked into the yard with his coworkers, James and Nate, this morning. He was in a horrible car accident. He totaled his car. I guess his coworkers found him in a ditch, hours after the accident, and brought him home. Driving like a crazy person was going to catch up to him someday, so I guess I shouldn't be surprised. I'm just surprised at the timing.

"Maybe the fates are conveying the time for trying to work it out has passed? At least that was my thought when the three of them walked into the garden," I choke out. Tears start to fall down my cheeks into the garden bed as I pace. The pumpkin vines blossom in my wake leaving a sea of yellow flowers.

"It just happened to be his two friends from work who found him. I think there's more to this than you realize, Alison. I think there was a reason he was flying home with those two nipping at his heels," she says thoughtfully.

"The car accident wasn't staged. Grant loves that car. He would never total it to cover up going to a bar. Plus, he looked really beat up from the accident, a split lip, and concussion," I say.

"There are no bars in Strawberry. Nate and James were leaving Paulino's when Grant left. How were you able to assess him for a concussion? James and Nate didn't tell you they went to a hospital, did they? James would have called Gran first, then I would have heard about it and called you immediately," Rosie says distantly.

I sit on the edge of the raised bed and take a deep breath. I don't want to talk about my private moment with Grant to find out it wasn't real. However, if I don't tell her then she can't help me interpret his odd behavior.

"I don't even know what goes into a concussion evaluation, but his personality was radically different. A concussion was the only explanation I can imagine for his complete change in attitude. Even his body language seemed like it belonged to someone else," I say through the tears. The tears puddle in a blossom that sprouts a small pumpkin in the center.

"Oh Honey, I'm so sorry. How was he acting differently? He didn't strike you, did he? Were James and Nate helpful?" Rosie says gently.

"No, nothing like that. He was only hostile to Nate and James. When James insisted they all return to Bergan, I thought Grant was going to kill him. When they were leaving, Grant kissed me and not the usual peck either. He devoured my mouth after undressing me with his eyes.

"If they wouldn't have rushed back to Bergan, Grant and I could have had a breakthrough," I say with a tear punctuating each word. I bow my head to wipe my nose. Did the pumpkin at my feet grow when my tear hit it? It is now orange and the size of a baseball.

"Increased hostility toward males with increased sexual aggression toward you…could it be? After the kiss, what was the look on his face?" Rosie asks. Each word is faster than the previous one and I can feel her excitement building.

"He looked like he was ready to tear my clothes off despite the fact we were standing in our open front doorway with Nate and James at our sides. See? Totally out of character. Wherever he was before coming home, is the source of his libido increase. If I were smart, I would just end it, but I long to be with him. It hurts to say that. Rosie, I love him," I cry.

"Then you need to be with him. I need to make a phone call before I can make promises, but I have a feeling he's more committed to you than ever. It's not cheating and not a concussion if I'm right. You need to hang on until I am sure," Rosie says.

Her kind words and excited tone inflate a bubble of hope in my chest. The tears stop and I stand to find a bowling ball-sized pumpkin next to my seat. Who could she be calling? No one knows Grant better than me, especially anyone in Strawberry. We have only lived here for a few months.

"Alison, have you been crying over this?" Rosie asks.

"Yes, crying over the garden all morning. I have made a mess of the pumpkin beds…"

"Are you still outside?"

"Yes, I thought I would…"

"Go. In. Now," she shouts into the phone.

"Why? I'm alone…"

"You don't know that. Please run in, now," she continues to shout.

I turn and run up the stairs to the balcony. Once I close the door to the house, I ask, "Buttoned up tightly. What's going on?"

"You have spies around your house. You have to be careful having private conversations too close to the end of your yard," she stammers.

"What? That's ridiculous!"

"Ridiculous or not, promise me you won't cry outside anymore. Better yet, stop crying altogether. Come in tonight and I will have made my calls to have answers on Grant's condition for you."

"I can stop. I'm going to clean up anyway. Thanks, Rosie," I say hanging up. This town gets stranger by the week. Spies in a country town? Maybe Grant isn't the only one who lost their marbles last night.

Chapter 12

"Thanks for the show, Boss," Nate says as we start walking to where they left their motorcycles. James hits him on the back of the head, and they exchange a look.

"Huh?" I ask, lost in my own thoughts. I bet I have a big dumb smile on my face. I have her taste in my mouth from our goodbye kiss and it's stealing brain cells by the minute. I can't believe I did that, with an audience. The best part is Alison went along with it. She wasn't concussed, hypnotized, converted to a shifter, abducted by aliens or possessed by pod people.

On her own accord, she neither pushed me away nor fired scathing words as I had often feared. I had become so comfortable in my distance from her I forgot the passion we shared. Do I dare to consider bringing it back into our lives? With my new self, do I have a choice?

"Yeah, it looked like those black and white movies where the aliens try to suck the faces off the humans," Nate continues. Both guys laugh at my expense.

"I've been feeling really odd about her today," I mumble distantly.

"You mean that you're a horny bastard? That's a shifter trait but only your true mate will smell good enough to pounce. Good news. Your wife is your one true mate. It would suck to be saddled with a woman who stunk," James explains.

"Yeah, chicks in the office are going to reek to high heaven," Nate laughs.

"Great," I say, wondering how many more freaky side effects I must deal with now. I start a mental task list with asking about side effects at the top.

"Don't sound so glum. All your new shifter traits are ones embedded in your psyche. The parasite brings them to the forefront," says James.

"That means your power animal must be something annoying like a housefly, mosquito, or I've got it...James, are you a skunk?"

"No, and my animal self doesn't decide your animal self, so stop asking. You will still be yourself only a little extra."

"Yeah, you are still the grouchy, irritable," starts Nate.

"Don't forget cantankerous," quips James.

"Yes, the cantankerous, surly task-master you were yesterday," Nate jokes.

Lost in my own thoughts, I don't respond to their teasing. I climb awkwardly behind James onto the back of his bike. We speed off with Nate leading the way back to Bergan.

As we pass the site of the accident, I can't believe my eyes. It is completely cleaned up. There is no evidence of a crash, my car, or even that anyone has disturbed the area. I wonder if the reason Bergan gave me the car in the first place was because they had planned to crash it.

I hope it isn't totaled because I sold my old car before the move. I add a visit to Josh's Auto to my mental task list. At the very least, I want to get my house keys. If these guys think they could keep me from finishing my bathroom encounter with Alison, they are crazy.

When we arrive at Bergan, I head straight for my office. I place my duffle bag neatly in the corner closet. I pull out my notepad and begin writing my mental task list. I am getting comfortable in my desk chair when I look up to find Nate and James are standing in my doorway, staring at me. I finish writing my list before making eye contact. I have things I need to accomplish.

"Are you for real, dude?" Nate asks when our eyes meet. That earns him another glare from James. What is going on between those two? I don't have time to figure it out.

"What?" I ask in return.

"Once you get in this room, it's like a switch is flipped. You become all business. Is it a physical trigger? I mean you were unconscious a few hours ago," Nate says.

Wow, was it only a few hours ago? I freeze and look at my task list. All the weariness over what has happened hits me like a freight train.

James is the one to break the silence. "Here's what we are going to do. The three of us are going to hit the gym where you can ask questions about your transition. You can work off some of the testosterone building in your new predatory body while helping along your muscle reassignment. Then we will shower, eat and nap. Repeat the cycle. You will be experiencing hormonal highs and lows for the next twenty-four hours which will alternate between giving you energy and causing you to pass out. Brad gave us strict instructions to keep you here and help you through this."

"James and Frankie helped me through my

transition. You are in good hands," Nate adds.

"Turnings and transitions are my roles in the pack. It's what I do," James says while shrugging his shoulders.

Nate claps James on his shoulder and I am struck by the familiar image: Brad, in my office, clapping us on the shoulder in the same manner. It is a green light, secret handshake, or brotherhood gesture. I missed it then because I was so focused on getting Brad to agree to the generic drug proposal.

What other signs have I missed? I instantly feel nauseous as Alison's words haunt me. She would accuse me of not being present, not listening, and not seeing what's around me in most of our arguments in Ohio. I don't feel better when we reach the weight room. I haven't lifted since high school and even then, it was part of conditioning for the soccer team. I was only on that team for the scholarships.

Bergan has a state-of-the-art facility for its employees with locker rooms and a small indoor pool. It softens the blow when asking people to relocate to Strawberry. There is a row of treadmills, elliptical machines, rowing machines, and a virtual reality ski machine at the end. In the far mirrored corner, there is a shelf of yoga mats, bands, smaller free weights, mats, rollers, yoga balls, and medicine balls. We walk toward the opposite mirrored corner which has weightlifting machines, benches, and a rack of larger free weights.

Nate and James sit at two machines, side-by-side like it is their home away from home. I hesitantly go to the rack of free weights and grab a ten-pound weight. I remember some basic curls and lifts from high school gym class. I don't want to injure myself. Nate and

James are snickering to each other, but I am too tired to care. Let them have their fun at my expense. I will find my revenge when they least expect it. I plop onto the weight bench facing them to start bicep curls.

Lift and fly! The weight nearly pops me in the chin as my arm launches through the curling motion. I look at my co-workers with wide eyes.

"The great part about getting increased strength is you also get faster reflexes, so you have to work harder to injure yourself," James says, trying to contain his laughter. "Your body will continue to increase in mass until you reach the muscle to bone ratio of your power animal. Since fat and lazy animals are not common in nature, most people bulk up during the transition. The bulk ratio will give us a clue as to which animal form you possess. Brad is truly hoping for another wolf but another cat, like Nate, would be helpful too."

"Was that why I got the BMW? I'm aggressive at work so I deserve to be run off the road?"

"Please don't make us out to be the bad guys," Nate says, "we are exterminating Fae who abduct and eat people. The mission of Bergan is the same as when you interviewed. It is our scope that is larger."

"How do I know you are not eating people? I have seen your fangs."

"I could have eaten you although you probably taste of regulations and to-do lists."

"Ha ha," I say with an eye-roll.

"You joined Bergan to save the world," James says with his index finger pointed to my chest, "now you get to put your money where your mouth is. I bet you would be a tiger but maybe you are a chicken."

"Sorry to burst your bubble but I don't believe my

movements are smooth enough to be a cat. Alison says she can hear me empty my car after work before I open the door to the house," I say, going back to the weight rack.

"Yeah, but you said your wife has freaky senses. Maybe she can hear when a normal person wouldn't," James says.

I instantly see red. I grip the twenty-pound free weight until my knuckles turned white. I start to puff air through my nose and a growl vibrates in my chest.

"Hey, sorry, Dude," James says, casting his eyes downward. "I never knew you to be this sensitive about her."

"At least now we can text Brad we know you are a growling predator," Nate quips. He shoots me a huge smile and a thumbs up. The gesture slowly fades as he takes in my glare.

"All the more reason to stay away from her until you get your shifting under control. Strong urges and emotions literally bring out your animal. You could unintentionally maul her," James warns.

"Aggression, temper, growling, sex drive," I grouse and then ask after a few minutes of silence pass; "Are there any other surprises before I start sprouting pointy bits?" I am pumping the weight up and down in bicep curls at a vicious speed. However, I don't even feel the weight when a day ago I would have used two hands to move twenty pounds.

"Ironically your senses will be heightened so you will be a match for your wife on that front," Nate says contemplatively. When I glare at him, he adds: "Sorry, ixnay on the ifeway." He puts his hands up in a defensive stance and bows his head.

77

"I should be the one apologizing. We have had a rough time...for a long time...as in separate bedrooms for almost five years before I moved here alone for ten months. I really want to work things out with her. This could not have come at a worse time. I can't keep a secret from her. Not now," I say, raking my free hand through my hair.

"I know this is new," James says. "Once you fully transform, we will train you to control your shift and you can focus on her. She will still be there. She doesn't even have a job to fund an escape, right?"

"She will be physically there because of Henrik but we've been living like that for about a decade. We keep ourselves busy and have parallel lives. We keep tip-toeing around the fact we aren't acting like husband and wife but more like a joint merger," I say sourly, switching my curls to the other bicep.

"No offense but that's not what it looked like this morning," Nate says with a snicker.

"This morning I thought I died so I went for it," I explain. "You know, it's tough to go after her when there's a big chance she will push me away. I don't want to come across as creepy, pushy, or god...even rape-y. After the #MeToo movement, I don't want to get lumped in with harassing guys. I thought if I gave her space but tried to be nice, then she would come around. If she gave an inch, I would follow. In her words, one of the stipulations of moving here was: "working on us".

"She never went into details on what that was or what it meant, but she did move into the master suite I set up for us. I'm supposed to know the location of our new boundaries without any hints from her. She behaves in the same frosty manner as in Ohio. Also, I'm supposed to know when I'm being aggressive in a sexy way or aggressive in a criminal way. I want to kiss her and throttle her at the same time."

"Dude, I never knew you had issues at home. You seem all business at Bergan, so it was assumed home was buttoned up tight," James says wiping a hand down his face.

"You don't get it because you aren't married," I grouse.

"But I am," says a voice behind me. Brad stands in the doorway. "I know this is extreme, but we are at war in this town. I hired you for your leadership skills not to get drug approvals. Our pack leader, Frankie, died in the last of the Fae battles. Now the Fae have a fortress in this realm, right at the edge of our city. Our need to get rid of them is stronger than anything else."

"We are at war and the human authorities haven't noticed? With social media and camera phones, that is impossible," I say.

"I believe the Fae would like nothing more than worldwide exposure. Fear and depression draw them. Disbelief gives them the opportunity to snatch victims. The Strawberry shifters have worked for over one hundred years to contain the problem to a remote area to avoid mass casualties." Brad's words ring true as he stares me down. Even if the jokers in IT are full of it, I believe in Brad's mission.

"I believe you. I'm on board but why me?"

"I felt bringing you, bringing your family, to Strawberry would supply us with a new leader. I'm sorry if you feel misled but I didn't know what to do."

"As CEO, aren't you the leader?" I hear my mouth

say. I can't believe I just said that. The shock must have registered on my face because three faces break into laughter at me.

"I'm the lightning rod," Brad explains with an apologetic smile. "As CEO of Bergan, I'm the one in the public eye. I bring in money and talent by moving Bergan with the times. It is a new pharmaceutical company because it was a telecommunications firm before that, a car part manufacturing plant before that, a grain mill and processing plant before that, you get the picture. Everyone is gunning for me. I keep the attention away from our real leader who, until recently, was Frankie."

"I wondered how a pizza parlor owner had a seat on the board of directors. I thought he was a retired chemist who made pizza for fun," I say, rubbing my temples. This is too much.

"Frankie was brilliant. He had the mark of the destined leader, the ability to partial shift," Brad says. The last question is directed to my bodybuilding chaperones. "Does Grant have it too?"

"He hasn't attempted a shift, partial or otherwise. He growled at us though," Nate answers.

"A predator is very useful but let me know when you start shifting lessons. I want to see a partial shift attempt," Brad directs them. I must have looked as confused as I felt because he adds in my direction: "The destined leader can stop his shift in the middle of the transition, so he has just a claw, just a muzzle of fangs, or just faster hind legs while the rest of his body is in human form. If his predestined mate is a shifter, then the mate can partially shift as well."

"We know his wife is his mate, even though she's

just a human," James says. My babysitters exchange a grin at that remark.

"What?! His mate is the recluse? Has he smelled her yet?" Brad asks.

"Yeah, she passed the smell test with flying colors," Nate says with a chuckle.

Both Brad and I shoot him a glare at that one. "She's not a recluse. It's easier to keep her at home. She has sensory processing disorder. Her heightened senses make things like buzzing fluorescent lights really painful."

"Well, she should fit right in here," Brad says waving a hand at us. "Everyone in this room has heightened senses. Whose idea is it to keep her at home?"

My jaw drops, which is all the answer he seems to need. He continues after a pause. "Frankie's sons are six wolf pups who, so far, cannot partially shift. The youngest two still haven't transitioned, however, their personalities are beta not alpha male. Rosie was more confident in her older sons being a leader, especially Frank Junior. Unfortunately, he can't do it."

"Alison spends a lot of time with them," I say setting my weight back in its rack, "I think she's homeschooling the younger boys with Henrik".

"That's a good place for her during the day," James says rolling his shoulders and neck. "Being surrounded by wolves is a great place to be if the Sluagh attack, particularly attached wolves like the boys will be to their teacher and friend."

"Looks like you guys have Grant under control. See that he stays here and call me if there's evidence of partial shifting. Welcome to Bergan, Grant, and this time, I mean it," Brad says smiling. He claps us on the shoulder one by one before leaving the gym.

The fact I am not feeling angry with him is a testament to how tired I am. I stand up and stretch. I watch James and Nate go wide-eyed and slack-jawed. "What?" I ask as soon as I stifle a yawn.

"Dude, your fingertips touch the ceiling now and your shirt is tearing in the middle," Nate gasps.

I looked down at my shirt to see holes developing in a vertical line up my sternum. I reach up to brush my fingertips to the ceiling. I am too tired to care. I stumble to the locker room and take a shower so hot my skin is red when I emerge. I find a Bergan sweat suit placed by my towel. It is a few sizes too big but who knows, maybe I'm a growing boy again? Nate and James are still pumping iron when I exit the locker room.

"There are bunks down here," James calls after me.

"Couch in my office," I reply without breaking my stride. I need to be alone to think. I desperately need to process and plan an escape from my jailers. However, all that will have to wait. I am asleep before my head hits my yellow couch cushions.

Chapter 13

I wake up to a wall of yellow. My face is tingling, due to the waffle weave printed on my cheek. I push myself to a sitting position from my spot on the floor facing the couch I fell asleep atop. If I'm going to be jilted in my sleep tonight, it's not going to be by an ugly yellow couch. Sleeping on the floor has made my every joint stiff, and the thought of going home makes another part of my anatomy stiff.

As I crawl over to my desk, the split cuffs of my sweatshirt dangle onto the floor. My neck is straining the head hole and the shirtwaist has managed to ride above my navel. I wrench the shirt around to try to make it fit to no avail. I use my desk to stand and the sweatpants suction to my legs like leggings. What is happening to me? I plop into my desk chair and get a groan in response from the chair. I have about had it. F-you chair. You too couch.

I start to scribble out a task list. I must see Alison. I am going to go crazy being stranded in here. I'm already feeling unbalanced from the overload of my new hormones. I focus on my list to hold onto my sanity. On my list, I need to call Josh, the auto shop owner, about getting my car keys. The car itself must be totaled but my key ring holds the keys to my house. I will probably be better off changing clothes before venturing out too. Will any of my clothes from home cover my larger frame? I add buying clothes online to my list.

I need to get the keys to one of the company vans to make my getaway. Finally, I need to physically get out of Bergan. I look down at my task list feeling confident in my plan. Then, I realize I had left a detailed outline of my plan for anyone to find. I'm definitely not James Bond material, I laugh to myself as I call Josh's Auto.

I let out a groan as I peek out of my office door to see the cube farm is a bustling pen of activity. I had forgotten about the night shift at Bergan, which works every alternating night from 10:00 pm to 6:00 am.

Outside my door, is a flurry of activity with dark-haired, pale-skinned clones walking, working and chatting. I was just praising Strawberry's twenty-four-hour activity when Josh had said his auto shop would be open all night, run by his friend—also named Josh.

Now I must matrix my way through the open area dressed like I've been marooned on a deserted island. I haven't met any of these people, but I sense they would tell Brad about my escape in a heartbeat. Mostly because a few days ago, I would have told on them too.

I rummage through my duffle bag for a miracle. My legs and arms are almost the same length, but they burst side seams in my pants and shirts. Great, I'm getting wider. With my luck, my power animal is a walrus or hippopotamus. My barrel-shaped chest is much wider too but at least nothing wobbles anymore, and my stomach is flat. I rip off the sleeves of an old college shirt and pair it with flimsy shorts.

Not only stylish but also great for the November weather. These are not going to work...unless...I use them to get to the gym where Bergan keeps sweats of all sizes to encourage team spirit. Adding an empty water bottle to my ensemble, I walk out of my office and strut toward the gym like I own the place. To my chagrin, no one looks my way and my hypothesis holds true—if you act like you belong then most people will just go along with it.

Check. Check. Check. I praise myself as I pull the giant 12-passenger Bergan van from the parking lot. I have my house key in hand thanks to Josh's friend Josh at Josh's Auto. I smile to myself at the absurdity of my situation and the repetition of the name Josh. The most amazing part of my caper is I am wearing a Bergan sweat suit that fits. There had been a set of shelves labeled "muscular sizes" which had wider arms at the biceps and shoulders. Why hadn't I noticed these accommodations before?

Probably because I hadn't entered the gym or the locker rooms since orientation. Every day at Bergan, I always went straight into my office only leaving it for meetings in the meeting rooms on the first floor. I found out the color of the carpet this morning and only because I had been thrown to the floor by a couch. What else have I been missing?

I get to see the entire town in detail because my sweet ride only goes fifty miles-per-hour at its top speed. It's a far cry from the BMW I am still mourning. Since Strawberry is the middle of nowhere, I get a great view of the night sky. Once I escape Bergan's parking lights, the stars twinkle brightly, and a waning moon guides my way. Alison loves looking at the night sky. For the brief period we dated, our dates were stargazing because quite frankly, we were broke college kids. I have always felt bad that I hadn't wined-and-dined her in those early days. However, her condition would have kept her from enjoying it, so I guess it's just as well.

My mind flashes images of her lying on the grass, gazing at the stars, pointing out different constellations and telling stories about the moon. We had been so happy then. I want nothing less than that happiness with her again, as soon as possible. With more income, we can have extravagant adventures. Whatever it takes, I can provide it to her now. I have made it to the top of the ladder in my field, maybe even top of the food chain. I push my foot harder on the gas pedal and instead of speeding up, the van begins to shake.

As I approach the curvaceous driveway, twenty minutes later, I am greeted by the majesty of our Tudor home. The grand arched entry is flanked by imposing turrets. Sheets of windows reflect the moonlight as if to defend against intruders with laser beams.

It was those windows that attracted my wife to the house. While I liked the isolation of the castle, she wanted a thinner barrier between her and the natural world. She has surrounded the house with an array of edible landscaping. It draws creatures of every size to our home. So much for isolation. At least our forest visitors won't ask me to help them edit a technical report.

I park the van at the base of my driveway and add it to my "F-you inanimate object list" with my desk chair and yellow couch. I jog along my driveway and use my phone to disengage our security system. All the windows in the giant renovated plantation home are dark and I get a rush from what I am about to do. Stupid because I am sneaking into my own house.

Mine. The word floats through my mind and I feel satisfaction warm my chest. The landscaping is in full bloom but that is Alison's domain. I remember her saying she planted nocturnal plants along with the regular ones so our house would have curb appeal twenty-four hours a day.

That had been in response to an argument where I accused her of bringing down our property value in Ohio with her giant gardens and hoop houses. I wince when I recall her face falling as I spat vile insults at her. As I walk around to the back of the house, I become cognizant of the gardens as an extension of her. They are more beautiful, and full of life in November than most are in July. Just like her.

Mine. The word keeps thundering through my brain as I creep through the house, up the stairs, and into our bedroom. I take a moment to look around as her citrus flowery scent teases my nose. The room is dominated by the giant bed, its mattresses almost four feet off the ground. There are flowerpots housing a single flower and slightly used candles on every surface. A crumpled flower petal sticks to the bottom of my foot. As I remove it, I see a few more petals stuck in the carpet threads.

A pile of red lacy cloth lays in the corner of the room as I move toward her side of the bed. I bend down to examine it. It is lingerie. I can't resist. I lift it to my face and inhale. *Mine.* My brain gleefully answers. She had put together a romantic night for us on Friday night. I instantly need to adjust my sweats as I am hard as a rock. She was saying yes to us, to me…and I hadn't come home that night. I stand up gingerly and let her lingerie drop to the floor.

Crack! I am hit across the back of my shoulder blades. I whirl around to find my wife armed with my old hockey stick. She is winding up for a second slash, so I must get my mouth moving. She looks magnificent though. Dressed only in one of my dress shirts, I can see the shadow of her curves in the moonlight. The golden stars in her eyes glow with angry fire. Even though her lips are pulled into a snarl their thickness is evident. The delicate pink bow is an object of my fantasies. *Mine.*

Crack! The stick blade hits the middle of my chest. Damn, my wife is strong. I stand there rubbing my chest waiting willing my breath back into my lungs. "It's me, Alison," I choke.

Thump! "Oh, I'm sorry," Alison stammers, dropping the stick to the floor. "You said you were staying the weekend at Bergan and then I heard someone enter. I was really scared so I got up and you were there. Only I didn't notice it was you and here we are," After looking at me closely, she adds, "You don't look like yourself."

"I don't feel like myself," I say quietly. I had hoped to mask my bodily changes with the cover of darkness. My plan to fool her isn't going to work. My wife is too sharp for that.

"Well, I'm glad it is you and not a serial killer," Alison says awkwardly.

Oh no, we are not going back to awkward. Surrounded by the evidence she wants more under her frosty demeanor, I am not going to let her get away. Not now. Never again. As soon as my queen realizes that our days of parallel lives are over, the better life will be for both of us. Too bad my mouth can't form words.

My eyes, however, possess a life of their own. They take in her red toenails at the end of delicate feet that are, for once, without traces of dirt. They follow her shapely legs to the bottom of the white dress shirt. It brushes at her upper thighs, so I use the moonlight to see the curves of her hips. I follow the curves to her tiny waist. It flares to her rib cage giving her torso the shape of a vase.

Atop her torso vase are her flowers, and her flowers are generous, almost too heavy for someone of her dainty bone structure. My hands itch to cup them as I blatantly stare. I watch her nipples pebble and my tongue becomes too large for my mouth. Her arms instantly cross over them, obstructing my view with red-tipped fingers.

"Well, now the threat of danger has passed. I'm going back to bed," she declares. However, she doesn't move. I try to give her a reassuring smile, but it feels a little too toothy. She has awoken the beast in me, and this has nothing to do with shifter blood. I can't control it now.

Chapter 14

He's staring at me so I shouldn't feel so stupid for just staring at him. His stare has touched every inch of my skin he can see and some that are thankfully hidden by my hasty choice in fighting armor. His face looks the same if you ignore the predatory smile. I have given the same smile to a bowl of ice cream. It is the "I found my prey" smile of satisfaction.

Below the smile, he is harder, squarer, not that I ever had issues with his dad-bod. However, it is evident he has been working out since we moved. *When does he have time for that?* I let my gaze travel over broad shoulders, hard planes and flat abs barely contained in a black sweatshirt. Completely out-of-control, I let my gaze travel down below his belt.

His pants are barely containing his erection too. My mouth waters at the flagpole between his thighs. It twitches back at me. Eek! Realizing I have been caught ogling him, I snap my eyes back to his face. I can feel my neck and face getting warm with embarrassment. The giant smile on his face isn't helping my composure, at all. Those blue eyes are smoldering again.

I can hear his heavy footfalls as he approaches me. It is the sound of power, size, and strength advancing right to me. My eyes are locked to his by a compulsion stronger than I can resist. I can feel the cold wall we have built between us melting away. This night is going to change everything. I am surprised by the fact I don't object. I will gladly exchange my safe place at arm's length for the hungry promise in his eyes. I just want him.

Like in the bathroom, he goes for my chin first, cupping it in his hands. This time there is no hesitation in his movement. His hands are steady and actions decisive. He brings our mouths together and sips at my lips. I open my mouth instantly to him in the hopes we can recreate our last encounter. He takes it as an invitation to plunder my mouth. *Did that moan just come out of my mouth?*

****

Alison's moan is music to my ears. I tilt her head to give me the best access to her mouth. I let my hands skim down her neck, rounding over her shoulders, urging her elbows to straighten. She allows me to place her hands on my shoulders, unintentionally granting me access to her curves, secrets, and treasures. I will not ignore this gift. Not tonight. I press her hands into my shoulders as a gesture to stay. I let my hands glide back to her shoulders, down her back to her ribs and around to her front.

I cup her heavy breasts. I knead and massage her breasts with a touch that is probably too rough, but I'm drunk on passion. She lets out a gasp and starts to back away, still holding my shoulders. I step into her space, so each step moves us as a unit until she gently hits the side of the bed. The bed is so tall the bottom of her rib cage is level with the top of the mattress.

****

Too much. Too much. Too much. My brain screams he is too much but at the same time, not enough. I need to get some space where his scent is not in my nose and his tongue is not in my mouth. I feel my back hit the bed and I'm caught in his trap. I'm embarrassingly aroused, practically throwing myself at him, soaking my panties in wanton fashion.

His hands push me until I'm bent backwards onto the bed. He steps closer to grind our hips together. There's no question in my mind his intention is to have sex tonight. The move puts some distance between our faces and I'm able to look into his eyes. The look in them takes my breath away. I see desire tangled with love. He's waiting. He's giving me time to reject him. His display of honor gives me the courage to take what I want.

****

Like two small birds, I watch her delicate hands flutter to the top button of the dress shirt she's wearing. She looks directly at my face as she slowly unfastens each button. I groan as her hands peel the two halves apart. Bent backward, she is laid before me like a feast. Her heavy breathing lifts her plump round breasts. Their tips point light pink nipples up to my mouth in offering. Her bare stomach a rolling meadow leading to tiny gray panties. The color is slightly darker in some areas than others telling me she's soaked them with her arousal.

I place my hand on her cheek and meet her gaze. I want her to see how precious this is to me. I let my hand trail lightly down her neck, breastbone, stomach to her panties. It must be my new shifter senses, but she smells of the garden after a spring rain. The more aroused she becomes the stronger it gets and the more intoxicated I get upon it. I sniff at the delicate hollow of her throat, hoping she doesn't get too weirded out by my animalistic behavior. I'm rewarded with her swallowing. I watch the muscles of her throat move and imagine the fun we could have using those.

****

Point of no return. Moment of truth. He either wants this or not. He is smelling me like I'm an exotic orchid and my mind starts to swirl with doubts and questions. I swallow them down and I watch his eyes light up as my throat muscles move. Fortunately, he doesn't linger and begins to feast on my nipples like a starving man.

The actions drive me up fast and I feel my legs opening involuntarily. He's alternating between drawing each peak into his mouth and thrashing each nipple with his tongue. My eyes roll back. My mouth hangs open in bliss as I let a wave of sensation wash over me.

****

She is already in a state of rapture, beautifully open to whatever I choose to do to her. The frosty wife I once had is nowhere to be seen. Little whimpers and gasps leave her lips to cheer me onward. I had forgotten how melodic those sounds were when I was too young to appreciate them. Her legs are stretched wide open and her wet core is rubbing on my pants. I hook my hands under each leg and lift her onto the bed. That's when I see them.

No. No. No. Not now. Not now. Long black claws curve from my shifter fingers. I focus on them and will the claws back in. My left hand complies but the claws on my right hand are defiantly staying out. Alison takes that moment to sit up and look right at me. I rip my sweatshirt over my head using my more human-looking hand and let it fall to the floor. I watch her eyes light up at my new larger chest. This worked but I need a bigger distraction.

I must slow down before I become a dangerously scary beast. Putting my good hand on her sternum, I press her back and bury my face between her legs. She jumps at the first contact of my cheeks to her inner thighs. Holding her in place, I let my tongue extend to taste all she is offering. My tongue is longer to accommodate the larger muzzle I am now sporting. I use it to my advantage and take her up fast. I use it to my advantage to pleasure her in innovative ways. Surrounded by her garden scent and melodic wails, I fight my new feral side and the need to dominate her. I feel a growl leave my chest and revel in it. *Mine.*

I let my eyes drift up her thrashing body. With her head thrown back, she has given up trying to stay civilized and is lost in the sensations washing over her body. I purposely make my breathing heavier to clear my mind and imagine myself as plain ordinary me. As my muzzle recedes, I must get moving before it happens again. I look at my hands and two normal hands are ready for use.

I kick off my pants and climb onto the bed beside her. My legs feel heavy and resist the tall step. That's when I look down and see they are as wide as Alison's waist and sprouting brown fur. *No. No. No.* I swivel her, so she lays lengthwise on the bed before me. I am so captivated I forget my transformation. I want to burn the image of her like this in my brain for all time. However, my more practical side reminds me one crack of her eyelids and she isn't going to be so compliant.

****

He made me see stars. This man sounds like my husband, but he is as much a stranger as the big shape I hit with the hockey stick. My husband has never worshipped my body like this. My body is pulsing to my own heartbeat like there is a rave inside of me. Had it been this way all those years ago? I don't think so. He was a boy then and now a man towers over me. A mature lover who reads my body like a manual.

His scent of warm spices fills my nose as he leans over to kiss me. I taste myself on his lips combined with the unique flavor of him and I groan. I am swiveled to face him as he climbs onto the bed. I feel his hands feather over me from face to knees. He has left no curve or hollow unexplored and he owns it all. I hear a rumble from his chest. No matter what tomorrow brings I feel myself bond tighter to him.

With no sweet words or coaxing, he wraps his arm around my waist and flips me onto my belly. He uses his strength to push my shoulders down, hoisting my ass into the air. I am completely open to this pose of submission. It is a physical manifestation of his ownership of me. I wait for his next move obediently and feel myself becoming more excited by the second.

****

Mine. The part of my brain that is turning into an animal has one purpose in mind—my wife's submission. I feel possessed as I flip her over and push her into a submissive pose. My knees kick her legs apart as far as they could go revealing all her treasures to the room. To my delight, she goes into position willingly and begins to pant with excitement again. She looks beautiful like this if only I could get her to start making those little whimpers again. I feel my muzzle start to elongate and I use it to run my tongue along her entire cleft. *Mission accomplished.*

I rise onto my knees behind her and gently glide into her. I stop to catch my breath and allow her to adjust to my invasion. I cannot abuse her trust and hurt her. She is so tight from our years apart and I vow not to let that happen again. I am going to be here inside her as often as I have her alone. My large heavy hips have a mind of their own as they brutally pound into her. She wails in rapture and I must work to keep my hands from becoming claws.

Her cheeks bounce with each thrust and I can't help watching them. I have always loved watching her curves, but this new angle is their best. If I let her head up, I could watch her breasts sway too, but I can't risk her getting an eyeful of my feral face. I am struggling to keep it together. I run my shortened fingers up her hips to cup each cheek. I watch her smaller pink entrance dance back and forth with each thrust. Like a man possessed, I reach forward to her to stimulate with my left hand, to gather the evidence of her arousal.

When she begins to push back on me in excitement my left thumb enters her. She screams and bucks harder, pushing back against me. I feel a fiery release building in the base of my spine as I watch her. Both of her entrances begin to spasm around me as she launches into a blinding orgasm. I follow her and release everything I had built up over the years into her. I slowly removed my thumb as she begins to shudder with aftershocks. I pump slowly until I am completely empty, and she has milked every drop from me.

I run a hand over my face. I am happy both my

hands and face feel completely human. My legs have shrunk too, I have mastered partial shifting and my wife. She lays curled into a puddle before me.

****

Um, what was that? My head is spinning, my vision is fuzzy, my voice is gone, and I am sore in places I didn't know could be sore. Who is this dominant man and how am I just learning about him now? My mind wants more of him, but my sore body would fall apart if I tried. I feel the mattress shift as he gets up, but I am too tired to see where he is going. I feel a warm washcloth between my legs and soft kisses feathering over my shoulder when he returns. His murmurings are urging me to sleep.

He lifts me as if I am light as a feather, so my head rests on my pillow. He tucks me under my half of the bedspread and curls around my back. His hands lightly smooth over my hair. This feels so perfect and I feel my body relax. My pulsing climax has finally stopped, leaving me feeling completely boneless.

****

Her breathing has slowed to a soothing rhythm while my body hums with satisfaction. If I stay another second, I am going to fall asleep. I must return to Bergan before James and Nate realize where I have gone. They must sense I am missing and could be searching the building already. I look down over my wife to decide if she is asleep. Long lashes rest on her cheeks in two dark crescents over her flushed cheeks. Her lips are bright pink and swollen from my rough kisses and I feel pride surge in my chest. I dampen it quickly, so my claws don't appear again. The reminder of my claws fuels my body to sit up. "Sleep deeply, my queen. I will come back to you when I can," I whisper in her ear. She doesn't respond or even move so I take that as a good sign she will not hear my hasty retreat.

****

With that, he just leaves. He came, got what he wanted, and then he just left. All the hope and love blooming in my heart starts to wither and die. I feel so used. My mind begins to travel down the darkest paths like a runaway train. Why doesn't he care enough to stay? If he used me now, who had he been using before? Hot tears drip down my cheeks to the pillow below. I can't heap all the blame onto him. I had pushed him away for years and tonight he gave me ample opportunities to push him away again. The truth is I want whatever he is willing to give me. *How pathetic*. This isn't how love works. Why can't he see that?

Chapter 15

The next morning the soreness in my body is dwarfed by the headache from crying myself to sleep. After a long bath in Epsom salts and juniper berries, I wash my face with a peppermint tincture to dull the pain and rub basil oil behind my ears to soothe my sinuses.

I can't be ill today as I'm teaching Henrik and the youngest Paulino boys. I hope Matteo, Anthony, and Tommy are more excited than Henrik to compare plants. Henrik's plant looks to be suffering but I do not dare touch it. I do not want it to miraculously grow overnight making him suspicious. Keeping my secret from Henrik, Grant, and the Paulino boys is getting more difficult as they pay more attention to me than anyone did previously.

"Alison, I thought I was better at science than math, but my plant has died," Anthony wails holding up his oregano plant. It had been a long, curly, green seedling when we looked at it last. Now, it is a grayish-green, stringy mess that flops along the side of the cup. Rosie's three youngest sons hold three identical cups with three identical dying plants. Henrik's cup doesn't look much better even though I had continuously reminded him throughout the weekend to care for it.

With a large tumbler of cranberry juice in hand, I'm watching five of the six Paulino boys while Rosie and Frank Junior are at Bergan. Since I help homeschool them several times per week, I'm glad to captain the ship. I love watching Henrik interact with the other boys. These deeper friendships are better than the acquaintances he had in school back in Ohio.

"Well in science, things go wrong all the time. As human beings we can't plan for everything, so we need to reflect on our actions, investigate, and fix the problem," I say in response. As I pull out a whiteboard and markers, Ray and Vinnie, Rosie's second and third sons, exchange a snicker at the folly of the younger boys. I glare over at them. "Aren't you two supposed to be trimming and blanching all the basil I brought with me? If it turns brown, I have photos to show your mom that it was green when I left it in your care," I call toward the kitchen.

"Sorry, yeah sorry," they mumble as they disappear into the restaurant's kitchen, keeping the door open. I smile to myself. The two self-proclaimed men-who-are too-old-for-growing-plants-in-cups are eavesdropping. They silently get to their tasks so as not to interrupt their brothers. They have a huge kitchen to work and they are cluttered in the two-foot counter space closest to the door.

"I don't think your plants are completely dead. If you want to try to save them, I think it's worth it. Let's start investigating. When we went over their care, we made a list of care instructions. Did you follow them?" I ask. I get four enthusiastic nods in response.

"Did you put them in the same window side-by-side, or did you use different windows?" I ask.

"Matteo and I put our cups in our bedroom window side-by-side," Anthony answers. Matteo doesn't say a word, not surprising since I think I've only heard him say four words in the weeks I have known him.

"Which direction does your window face?" I ask.

"The street", replies Anthony. I hear giggles from the kitchen. The younger boys don't seem to hear the giggles, so I let it go.

"Your room faces east like mine," says Henrik, "that's why I put my cup in our kitchen, which faces south. I know the east has the best sun in the morning so it's super cold there. West would only get evening sun but in the south or north, the plants get a little sun all day." I record the data he gives on the whiteboard.

I turn to Tommy, the youngest. "Where did you put your cup? We can help you find the direction the window faces," I ask him gently.

"I didn't put it in a window at all," he wails. "I left it out on my bedside table so I would give it care first thing every morning. I knew it was dying but I didn't know what to do. I think these plants are defective."

I write his data on the whiteboard. I repeat this process with the amount of watering, type of water used, temperature of the water, and the estimated temperature of the room where the plants were kept. I was impressed with the boys' diligence in caring for their seedlings. I could tell they were very distressed over their results, especially Tommy. By the time the data is recorded, they are all pleading and wailing it is not their fault, but the seedlings are defective.

"Looking at the data, we have an excellent experiment and you should be proud of what you have done," I start. The boys are looking at me as if I have grown an additional head, so I continue. "All of you started your plant using the same procedure and then followed your care instructions exactly. You gave them standardized care, so they are easy to measure and compare. However, Tommy brought up a good point. During the experiment, he noticed the care instructions were not what the plant needed. Even though he realized this, he kept treating it the same way."

"I didn't know what to do. You weren't here to ask, Mom was too busy, and when I asked Frank, he didn't know either. I wish Dad were here. He could have helped," Tommy says. Anthony pulls him into a hug and pats his shoulder.

After a pause I ask: "When we planted them, did you each do the exact same thing?"

"No, I have two cups because I got a hole in mine," Anthony volunteers.

"I didn't put a lot of soil because I didn't like the feel of it under my nails. My plant is shorter than everyone else's plant," says Henrik.

"I broke the stem on this part. I don't know how, maybe it was that way when you gave it to me," Tommy says suspiciously. I hear more giggling from the kitchen.

"So, each of you accommodated your plant to fit their needs," I say. "You recognized it wasn't the plant's fault that it had a cup with a hole, a shallow dirt bed or a broken stem. Instead of following my lead, you did what would give your plant the best success. Let's compare what you did on day one to the rest of the time. Did any of you modify the instructions once your plant started to suffer?" Four heads slowly shake in response. Tommy has tears in his eyes.

I keep talking to keep him from wailing again. "When you are taking care of something or someone, you can't just set it aside and hope everything works out. You need to check-in often and really see what is going on. If your plan is not working, then you need to change the environment not necessarily the plant itself. Anyone can plant a plant, but it takes constant work and care to grow one.

"When you check-in and it is not thriving, it takes a lot of courage to change the way you take care of your plant. This is especially hard if the care is written instructions or you have taken care of it that way for so long. The care instructions become a form of habit. Let's look closer at the plants." I pull out a set of magnifying glasses and direct the boys to use them to look at the bottom of the leaves.

"When I look under the leaves, my stomata are closed but the lips are really thin," Henrik says leaning over the table.

He is answered by a chorus of "mine is too" from the other four boys.

We brainstorm what is happening and agree to give the plants clear soda. I explain the soda will give them sugar, electrolytes, carbonation and most importantly moisture. "This is not what you expected would fix them, right?"

"No, this is weird," says Anthony crinkling his nose.

"Sometimes a plant needs special care, which means they need resources that may seem weird. It doesn't mean the plant is defective. Each plant has special conditions that help it to be the most beautiful plant it can be. Some conditions are standard like sunlight, soil, and water; others are more specialized like grow lamps, plant food, and hydroponic solutions.

It shows we care when we get it the mix of conditions correct and support them. Not just at the beginning but throughout their lives." Or

Tommy squeals, "Or until we eat them!"

On that note, I decide they have had enough philosophy for one day. We decide to cut off the broken part of Tommy's plant. We repot Henrik and Anthony's plants, so they have bigger cups with new soil. After the plants are settled in their new pots, I tell the boys to go wash up before helping in the kitchen. Left alone, I can finally touch the plants.

I'm checking the root system of each of the boy's plants by gently lifting them out of their cups and they are already trying to stand again. I smile with relief. They have been saved by the extra attention from their owners. Cleaning up the spilled potting soil, I can peek under my elbow to catch a glimpse of who is shuffling behind me. It is the two older boys hesitantly approaching the table.

"When you first talked about plants in cups, we thought it was a little kid thing. However, you were talking like adults," Ray says to his toes.

"Yeah, you were talking about life, right?" Vinnie asks.

I look at both boys and see their dilemma. Without their father, they are being asked to do more and grow faster. The fifteen- and seventeen-year-old are so close to adulthood that it would be easy to ask them to carry more than they are capable of carrying.

Frank Junior has stepped into his father's shoes in taking care of the ordering, dealing with suppliers, and accounts, and the other financial aspects of the business. This leaves his former chores in the business vacant. While the two boys before me can take care of carrying loads of vegetables from the trucks for their brother, they haven't reached the maturity to take on the other roles.

"Hopefully, the younger boys learn about taking care of their family someday. I'm sure they will be caring and responsible husbands and fathers. You know, I brought backup plants in case they had truly killed the first set. These backup plants might not make the trip back to my hoop house…" I say to test their reaction. I see the hope in their eyes and small smiles start to form. I see both boys have a dimple in their left cheek. They are always so serious I can't recall ever seeing it before now.

Ray speaks for the pair, "Could you help us with our own plants? I mean, apart from the little boys, help us too?"

"I think that's a fantastic idea," I say. "Naturally, we would meet without them since you two have had more science classes. If you can find some cups to transplant this mass to give them extra space, we can start right now."

"I remember where we have extra paper Christmas cups. Mom won't mind if we use those," Vinnie says while scampering off to the kitchen. I see a glimpse of the child he was a few months ago, before his father's passing. I feel honored to bring him a few seconds of youthful joy and be the one he feels safe enough around to let it show.

I look to Ray and see the circles under his eyes. He's quiet and mild-mannered like Matteo but has had to push his boundaries to fill Frank Junior's shoes. Rosie has told me about his anxiety about running the register and talking to everyone, even though everyone in the town has watched him grow up.

"How much did you guys hear from the kitchen?"

"We didn't mean to eavesdrop. It was just kinda boring sifting through basil stems," Ray says to his shoes.

"I'm not mad. I don't want to bore you further by repeating it," I say gently.

"It was cool to think about how to take care of everyone individually," Ray says. "I got to thinking about how Matteo turns off the overhead lights and lights the table lamps when we know you are coming. We should all be doing stuff like that for each other."

I'm touched Matteo, who doesn't talk to me, accommodates me without anyone asking. "There are many ways to show someone you care. These are called accommodations and are commonly needed to make others comfortable," I say.

"Is that because you have a sensor disease? Mom told us she enjoys finding combinations to make sauces that you will eat because if you will eat it, then it will be the talk of the town. She says you have a supertaster tongue."

I can feel myself tearing up and find I must swallow a few times before replying. "It is called sensory processing disorder, so yeah, I have super sensitive taste buds. I can also hear the lights buzzing, the coolers singing, and the giggles coming from the kitchen."

"That would be so cool…"

"Most of the time it is, but I need my accommodations to be comfortable."

"Like turning down the lights or giving soda to

plants."

Vinnie returns and the three of us get lost in setting up the plants. I let my mind wander toward Grant and his way of accommodating me in our marriage. By having a few conversations, the boys have learned to accommodate me without seeing me as less of a person. If I could have the same rational conversation with Grant, would he get it? The problem is when he enters a room, I become lost to the emotions swirling around us. Our history has been sabotaging our future.

Our past is so heavy. Frankly, our present is heavy too but with confusion. He oscillates between being passionate and being not just distant like before but totally gone. No wonder I only feel gratitude that he has chosen to spend time with us instead of anger that he is toying with me like a yo-yo. I start to formulate what to say to him when he comes home tonight...if he comes home tonight.

Chapter 16

If Nate or James are savvy to my excursion, they aren't letting on. For the last thirty hours or so, I have been a good little soldier much to their collective amazement: workout for an hour, shower, eat and then four hours of sleep on my yellow nemesis. Rinse. Repeat. I have filled out rapidly due to the constant workouts until now I am as bulky as I am tall. I ordered business suits sized for bodybuilders and can only hope they will be delivered to Bergan today.

My changing body aches as if I have been run over by a bulldozer. I eat everything not nailed down while Nate delicately picks at barely cooked steaks. My stomach seems to be constantly empty. I attribute my appetite to my increased bulk. James has expressed it means that my power animal is big. I have decided to keep my partial shifting to myself, so I don't accidentally give away my secret trip home. My dreams are lust-fueled scenes starring my wife with little variation on the theme.

Finally, Monday arrives with the relief of normalcy. I look at my task list that I had left on Friday evening and it seems more significant now I am aware of the whole picture. Understanding that Bergan is the funding for a larger agenda makes me even more proud of my role in the submissions. My inbox holds a message from Brad announcing a pizza lunch for the

Azolicyst win. I am so excited to congratulate the members of my team and I can probably eat a few pizzas on my own.

"Grant, do you have a minute?" I hear Patty, my most senior employee, ask from my doorway. She stays put in the doorway with downcast eyes until I respond. Patty is average height, average build, with average brown hair and with average brown eyes. She is a self-proclaimed hermit with an eye for detail. The combination is perfect for a regulatory affairs specialist because most of her time is spent editing and organizing documents by others. The job isn't glamorous, but neither is she, especially when I compare her to my fiery redhead at home.

"Come in and sit a second," I say, "I want to warn you I am going to thank everyone individually on the Azolicyst formally at lunch today. I'm writing a little speech—"

"Please don't," Patty starts as she approaches my desk. The smell hits me before she reaches my guest chairs. I must have made a face because Patty freezes to study me. I watch her eyes dart around as she takes in my appearance. I had hoped to conceal my new size behind my desk, but Patty misses nothing. She reaches out, grabs the guest chair, and pulls it to where she has stopped. She fans out her long sweater jacket and flips her hair as she sits.

"You will want to move these chairs closer to the doorway now. Brad has them on the opposite wall from his desk. We have to shout across the room to talk but at least he doesn't make that face at me," she says when she's settled.

My jaw drops to my desk. Could she know? Had I

failed to keep the company secret from the first person I encounter? The silence stretches on as my mind races from surprise to guilt to frustration. I fail to form the correct words to diffuse the situation as she stares at me. I need to get it together.

"Of course," she adds, giving me a pointed look, "If you add a coffee table between the two chairs, it would feel less awkward."

"Good idea. Please put ordering a coffee table on a task list for the next intern," I say, once my composure returns.

"I wanted to see you about the generic. Did you get a green light from Brad?"

"Yes, he agreed it is easy money," I reply, grabbing my markers. "I outlined how the ANDA would be easier than the NDA for Azolicyst had been." Patty and I spend hours diagramming the strategy, creating a timeline, assigning tasks to different people and defining her role in managing the project.

During the power session, a tower of delivery boxes arrives and my confidence soars. It feels so comforting to be back in my wheelhouse of pharmaceuticals rather than paranormal battles. However, I purposely leave myself out of the project when I want to oversee it all. I will act as a consultant to support Patty as the lead. Not only do I wish to measure her leadership abilities, but I also need to keep myself free for larger projects. I have a war to fight.

I dismiss Patty to check up with the chemists on their project set up and email the microbiologists to adjust their lab space. Since I had contacted them previously, they should have methods, SOPs—standard operating procedures—and supply requests for Patty to review. They are going to have three projects going at once and it was imperative everything is kept in separate spaces.

The Bergan microbiologists are part of the company that only works at night. Their hours are one of the secrets behind our success. Generating data at night so it can be analyzed during the day, means we are twice as productive as any other company.

Check. Check. Check. That meeting with Patty checks off many pieces from my task list. I open my Amazon boxes to find my order complete: shirts, pants, belt, undershirts, boxers and a giant bag of dried cranberries. Even though my stomach will gladly accept anything I wish to eat, berries have become a favorite. I quickly change into a set of clothes that match the only dress shoes I have in my office.

I may have a wrinkly pattern of squares on me but at least I will no longer be confined to wearing a sweat suit. Feeling much more like myself, I sit down to my task list. Most of it is asking Brad more about the war and the frequency of the attacks. I must corner him after lunch.

"We got lunch catered in! We got lunch catered in! We got lunch catered in," Nate and James sing in unison as they conga into my office. I must laugh at the dancing pair. Hunched over validation reports, I manage to make a sizable dent in the next NDA which still has months before it is off stability testing. After physically checking off items on my task list, I rise to follow them to the party.

"What are you supposed to be, a raisin?" James jokes.

"No, he's more like a prune, pushing out as much

data as he does," Nate quips.

I use my non-dominant fist to punch Nate in the shoulder and get rewarded with a jovial yelp. The three of us laugh and push each other down to the meeting rooms. We find the room unerringly by using our advanced sense of smell. It immediately reminds me of Alison.

She would hate being bombarded by the mix of smells inhabiting a cube farm. Days like this, where a catered lunch brings a dominant smell to the office, would be a relief to her. It reminds me of how she avoided the cafeteria in college like a quarantined hospital ward. I work as much as I do so she can stay home in comfort with Henrik.

When I walk into the meeting room, the room is divided by gender. Had every meeting been this way and I hadn't noticed? Even Rosie and Frank Junior are setting up identical buffet lines on opposite sides of the room, each with their respective gender. I zero in on Frank Junior's buffet line, charge over and begin to pile Italian food on my plate.

"You will want to grab some of the tortellini salad," Frank says with a huge grin.

"Oh yeah, is it the best thing going?" I ask.

"Well, it was folded by Henrik," Frank replies.

"Really? I had no idea he had an interest in cooking," I reply.

"I wouldn't say it is an interest but Mom gives everyone jobs during the closed hours so she can have lunch with Alison. Alison comes over some days to teach math and science while Mom teaches Italian. Once Mom learned Henrik's piano fingers could fold tortellini at the speed of light, she adopted him into the business," Frank says, barely containing his laughter.

"I imagine as long as your mom feeds him and lets him play the piano to your customers, it's a fair trade," I reply while scooping out a giant portion of tortellini onto my already full plate. It feels great to get good reports on Henrik. Back in Ohio, it seemed like he was getting disciplinary reports every day. I am pleased my family is making friends with another family while I am working. I wonder how Alison can visit the restaurant for extended periods of time with the fluorescent lighting and buzzing coolers.

"All this tasty grub and you make a plate looking like lawn clippings. What? Are you watching your figure?" I joke as Nate and I join James at a table.

"F-off," James grouses. "I'm a vegetarian."

"Just kidding, geez. You should taste the tortellini. Cheese and green stuff filling instead of meat and rolled by my son," I reply.

"He's just sensitive about the limits placed on him by his inner self," Nate says.

"I've been warned," I say with my hands lifted in surrender. "I need to stay on your good side because I have some more questions about, you know, my inner self," I add making quotation marks with my fingers.

"Fire away, then," says Brad as he joins our table. I stop to look at him. It is so hard not to think of him as my boss. I remind myself he's the CEO of Bergan because he's not the leader of the pack of shifters.

"I want to ask you for some time to discuss more specifics on our common enemy, you know, to our town," I hint to Brad.

"Why wouldn't you ask now? Everyone in this room is a shifter and awaiting a leader. Did you ever partially shift?" Brad says loudly.

"Like this?" I ask morphing my left hand into a big hairy paw with long black claws. I use my index claw to spear a cherry tomato from James's plate and pop it into my mouth. Three sets of giant eyes watch me in stunned silence.

"Did you see that folks? Our leader has arrived," Brad announces to the room. Then directly to me, he adds: "This party is a welcome to the family. We are here to catch you up to speed so you can help lead us against the Fae." The room erupts into cheers and applause. I can only look around in amazement.

"Congrats, dude," says Nate. I exchange high fives with them as well as Frank Junior who is checking on the table.

"It's a big job. Make sure you involve everyone who has offered to help, in whatever way they can help," James says ominously.

"So, tell me about the Fae. What makes some little fairies so dangerous?" I ask the table after the room's applause dies down.

Little fairies," Nate says followed by a snicker.

"The Fae are fairies in their own realm. They come to this realm as Sluagh for punishment when they don't abide by the Fae laws. Sluagh suck blood, eat hearts, and steal souls to stay young. They are the monsters who go bump in the night. Their grotesque bodies are armed with black claws, acidic black saliva, and giant beautiful wings. The wings have shimmering colored panels that turn gray when they die but stay beautiful until the end," James says.

"So, they are like butterfly vampire hybrids?" I ask.

"Not at all. The vampires are on our side, including my wife, Molina. Since you didn't know, I'll let it slide but don't let her catch you comparing her to the Fae," Brad says, frowning at me.

"I'm sorry. No offense was meant by that," I say, retreating into my seat.

"Again, no problem. There's no way you could have known our night staff is made completely of vampires. I work the afternoons and half the evenings to run both teams but Ryan, the quality assurance manager, manages them when Molina or I am not there," Brad explains. The surprise is evident on my face as my jaw drops.

"For such a genius, I always wondered why you never questioned why Bergan has a blood bank," James says to me.

"Bloodborne pathogens was my guess," I reply quickly. I watch the smile fall from his face. Why do I get the feeling he is in competition with me? What is his deal?

"The Fae love to capture us because we have double souls. The part of us that is human and then the extra side dish of our power animal. We are like a whole combo meal instead of just a sandwich," says Nate.

"Yeah and a witch would be a combo with dessert," says Rosie, approaching our table, bringing with her a cloud of garlic.

"They are triple souls because they have their human part, an inner power animal, and a piece of mother earth. Triple souls can be used to bargain their way back into the Fae, so Sluagh want them the most. That's why we rarely call Rosie's boys to arms when the Fae attack. Rafaella, their grandmother, is the most attacked person in our town. We leave all six boys to protect her," Brad says.

"I have been very grateful Brad and my Frankie have that policy. I had hoped Grant will continue to honor it, unless he wants to take a few of my boys to guard his family as well. The boys are very attached to them. Perhaps during the next new moon, Alison and Henrik could stay with us. That way the boys only have to defend one place," Rosie says to me meekly.

I was more surprised by her change in demeanor than her request. Where is the loudmouth who bosses everyone around the pizza parlor? Is she intimidated by being surrounded by pharmaceutical professionals? "I need to see the metrics where our resources lie before I start making promises. It makes sense. Your boys are needed to guard their grandmother. Alison and Henrik will stay inside at night. They barely leave the house anyway, so guarding them beyond our security system will not be necessary," I say cautiously.

Rosie casts her eyes down. I feel like she has more to say but for some reason, is holding it in. After a few moments of trying to meet her gaze, I ask, "Is there more?"

"You don't think the Sluagh are going to go after Henrik and Alison?"

"This first attack will not be directed at them," I say. "There's no way the Sluagh would know I'm the new leader so there's not a reason to single them out. Once they attack and find out, we will need to reconvene to include them. However, if we can defeat the Fae in one battle, it's a non-issue."

"Defeat them in one battle? Are you kidding? We

don't even understand how they keep getting into our realm. It would be smarter not to underestimate these monsters. They are fighting for survival too," James says, getting up to leave. He stomps out of the room.

"Great job Sarge," Nate quips. "The first hour on the job and you piss off your oldest officer."

"What?! I thought you were the senior one!" I say in amazement to Brad.

"Nope, the lightning rod, remember?" he replies with a sad smile.

"Don't worry about him. He did the same thing to Frankie. He will support you on the battlefield and respect you after your first win," Rosie says, leaving the table to check on the other guests. Thankfully, she takes her garlicky aroma with her.

"The addition of a Fae prison tells me they want a place to stay with a steady food source. I think they want to make Kentucky their landfill forever," Brad says.

"They would want a steady stream of revenue to do that. They will attack Bergan next, probably during the vampire shift. Then, when we arrive for work the next day, it's like grocery delivery. If we can set up a defensive trap around our building, we can take them out using home-field advantage," I say, thinking out loud.

Frank Junior straightens from the chair he was leaning against to ask, "What would the Fae need money for?"

"Money makes the world go 'round," I reply standing up.

"Do you want to sketch out a plan for the New Moon? Everyone can tell you where Frankie had them

117

in the last battle," Brad says.

"You mean the last battle where we lost. If I am a destined leader then I can figure this out without losing anyone," I say. I refill my plate and take it back to my office. I'm fired up. Ideas on how to save our town swirl in my head. I take a photo of the ANDA meeting notes on my whiteboard to send it to the cube farm printer. As the printer sputters and spurts, I wipe down the board. I draw, write and plan as the hours fly past. Before I know it, the sun has set and it's after 9 pm. I didn't come home...again. The only question now is which is more important, to finish this plan, or to check on my wife?

Chapter 17

Cheetah I am not, I say to myself while puffing up my driveway with a duffle bag of my new clothes. I had started walking home only to turn back to Bergan to grab one of their vans. It rattles so loudly it sounds like a marching band heading for my house. I must leave it at the end of the drive and finish my journey home on foot as to not wake up my entire household.

My inner beast is definitely neither speedy nor migratory. Maybe it just sits in the trees all day like a sloth. I wonder if I'm a giant sloth—like the ones from the Pleistocene epoch. I never asked Nate if anyone is an animal previously thought to be extinct. I put that on my mental task list.

As I follow a curve in the driveway, I decide to cut through the trees. Walking in a straight line means fewer steps and right now, I'm ready to sleep in the woods. As I navigate the small forest, the motion-activated lights pop on in the back of the house. Instantly my vision goes red and a growl rumbles from my chest. I try my best to be silent as I sneak around the hoop house array my wife has set up in the backyard.

I am naturally loud, but my increased mass has made my footfalls thunderous. I sniff the air and find that earthy citrus I love. What is she doing outside? Is she alone or is there someone else dragging her outside? I quicken my footsteps and reach the backyard in time for the lights to go out.

When the land behind our house was leveled, the original house builders piled it in front of the house. This causes our basement to be a walk-out lower level and our main floor to be a story above the elevation of the land in the back of the house. To compensate for this, one of the homeowners along the way built large balconies off the kitchen on the main floor and the master bedroom on the top floor. The balcony of the master bedroom is barely ten square feet in area while the kitchen balcony is close to two hundred square feet. Each balcony is ringed with a 3-foot-tall railing topped with a wide ledge.

Perched on the ledge is Alison in some sort of yoga pose. She is so still the motion-sensing lights have turned off. Her skin glows in the moonlight, exposed by her tiny exercise outfit and pulled back hair. Her bare shoulders and arms lift the front of her body from where it is tucked against the ledge. The motion has pushed her breasts up and forward as they are smashed below her body. Long legs encased in silver skin-tight pants point upward and wrap around her form. They create a semicircle frame over her, ending in bare feet pointing over her head. Her eyes are closed, and her lips are parted to breathe gently so her body stays still. I find myself holding still too. She has a magical beauty out here and I'm captivated. I slowly lower myself to sit in the dirt under the tree.

Watching Alison in the dark, I'm completely caught off guard when a sleek black wolf sits beside me. Its coat is shining in the moonlight and its eyes are slightly glowing. "I would say this is weird or I'm scared you are going to bite me, but you are probably one of my co-workers. If you have come here to ogle my wife, I'll make your life a living hell," I whisper forcefully at the wolf.

The wolf is not impressed by my show of strength. It walks in a small circle, showing me all its sides and inadvertently its gender before curling into a ball beside me. She licks her paw at me with disdain. "I'm sorry. I guess you are not interested in being my competition for her. I jumped to that because I haven't been there for her recently, as I have been at Bergan going through my change. I had finally started to feel copacetic, and then decided to hike up my driveway," I whisper as I chuckle nervously.

Alison slowly lowers her legs to the ledge and uses them to push her hips up. I gape at the ripple of muscles beneath her skin. Was she always that strong? I look around at all the raised beds and hoop houses she must have built by herself. Maybe her muscular form is from that or maybe everyone is getting a little ripped. For a few seconds she wobbles, and she closes her eyes to get steady. I'm treated to a few seconds of her ass wiggling in the air.

My pants instantly become tight and uncomfortable. As I reach to adjust myself, I swear the wolf snickers at me. I give it a glare before returning my attention to Alison. She has lifted her torso so she's standing facing away from me with her legs far apart. She raises her arms to shoulder height and starts to go still again.

A movement across the yard catches my attention. We have one neighbor whose house sits beyond the hoop houses and the partially bare pumpkin fields.

Tonight, this neighbor is outside on his balcony

too…with binoculars. I feel a rumble in my chest and the wolf gets up to look around. She sniffs in the direction of the neighbor and turns back to me.

Swinging her head, she comes back to sitting at my side. The binoculars lock onto my position and we stare at each other for a while. "I take it from your body language you know that guy. I can't believe the nerve of him to blatantly watch her," I say gruffly to the wolf.

The wolf gives me another disapproving look and pushes her snout at my elbow. "Yeah, I know I'm just as bad. However, I'm married to her. I provide for her. I provide this house. I can gaze at what's mine, right?" I ask the wolf. I get a glare in response, not that I am expecting the wolf to answer.

I turn back to Alison. She has twisted her torso to look directly at one of the open gardens. It is full of short green plants straining back toward her. She narrows her eyes and jumps off the balcony, landing with ease. I cover my mouth to muffle my gasp as my heart jumps into my mouth with fear she wouldn't land well.

Alison reaches for the gardening apron left tied to one of the posts of the balcony as she stands. She ties it to her waist with practiced hands. A serene smile curves her luscious lips. It is a far cry from the frown I am used to receiving. "Well, what has made you wish to visit us? I can't have such a poison living amongst my greens. Your pollen could kill someone," she says, striding toward the raised bed.

The hairs on the back of my neck instantly stand on end. There is magic crackling in the air around her that I have never felt before tonight. I usually try to stay out of the gardens because it's the hobby to keep her busy while I'm away. Watching her in her element shows me a quiet power I never knew she possessed. Even the wolf has raised her head with her ears straining forward and eyes glowing in the darkness.

The angle that Alison is walking directs her farther away, so she can't be talking to us. I raise up to my knees to see who she's addressing. She steps into the garden bed and walks down the center. New plant life sprouts in her footsteps and established plants grow fuller as she passes. It creates a green carpet in her wake with each leaf tilted toward her in worship. I am overcome with the urge to bow down to her too.

"Perhaps you would be welcome in another person's nightshade garden, but I'm growing an edible garden for my friends," Alison coos to a purple-flowered plant. "I can't endanger my friends, but I can give you a new home. Let me think about the perfect place for you to live and I will set you up there."

She bends down and scoops up the entire plant and tucks it into her apron pocket with a little dirt. The plant seems to lean against her body as she tucks it in lovingly. She hangs the apron on the post at the end of the garden bed with the plant-filled pocket facing outward. I watch her bend down to fuss with the apron pocket still whispering to the plant. I am captivated by her gentle ministrations.

Pleased with the plant's temporary home, she heads back to the house smiling at the plants. Again, the leaves on the rows of plants rotate to smile back at her. I suppress the urge to approach her and experience the magic radiating from her. This is her secret. She has never chosen to share this with me. A black void sits heavily in my chest.

Being on the other side, where she has a magical secret and an important place to be without me, feels like shit. I became a shifter less than a few weeks ago and she has been the plant whisperer forever, probably since birth. "Where have I been?" I murmur to the darkness.

I get a disapproving glare from my wolf companion. "You don't have to say it. I've been an egotistical ass to her, but you must see it from my side. I'm bringing lifesaving medicines to the human population and now saving the shifter race from the Fae invasion. I'm a good guy, really I am," I say to the wolf. The wolf snorts at me and pushes at my elbow to get me to stand up.

"I do need to face the music. As much as I'm loving her, she's pissed I'm still not racing home to see her each night. I can't come clean and betray the town's secret shifter population, but I can take the punishment from her to find some common ground.

"Moving here, I took her away from her job at the nursery and she didn't even complain. Maybe if I support her in building a nursery here...I don't know. I don't even know her hopes and dreams anymore," I babble to the darkness as I sling my duffle bag over my shoulder and walk to the front of the house.

Inside, I find her sitting on the bathroom counter with her feet in her side of the double sinks. She has changed into my old college fraternity T-shirt which hangs almost to her knees. She is hunched over in concentration, hands swirling in the water. She looks small again, not like Flidais presiding over her plant-based subjects at all. As I openly stare at her, I wonder if she's only powerful outdoors or if it's an elaborate cover-up because she knows I'm staring.

"Knock, knock. It's me. I'm home," I say at the doorway. I don't want to sneak up on her and get attacked by a hockey stick again.

"Hey," she says without turning toward me.

Oh no, we are not going back to frostiness. The last time we were together it was fiery passion and that's the way I plan to keep it. Even if she's spitting scorching curses at me, it's better than this cold hopelessness. I walk over to her and put my hand on her back. She instantly shakes it off and I frown at her. She doesn't see my expression because she has yet to look up from the water.

"Sorry, I missed dinner—"

"No problem. We are used to it," she murmurs to the water.

"Well, that's not right"

Her head snaps up and she stares right into my eyes. "Does it really bother you to be away? I always thought you preferred it."

I'm struck dumb. What kind of question is that? I'm trapped between wanting to tell her everything and just wanting to find amicable happiness with our mutual secrets. She pulls the drain on the sink and the muddy water spins down the pipes. Its similarity to this conversation hits me like a ton of bricks.

"I admit my job has been life-consuming. I remember the one promise you asked me to make with this move was to create more space for you in my life. Please hear me when I say, I want to spend every extra second I have with you."

"That's why I'm stuck though. Your intentions, words, and actions do not match. I can't read your mind to know what you want from me. You always say the right words to make me comply with your wishes as if you have studied pillow talk in your spare time. However, your actions speak volumes on how you prefer living apart from this family.

"I would set you free from your obligation to take care of us if I knew that was what you wanted. However, we go in circles when we talk so I don't know what to do. I'm lost in our marriage. I don't like feeling as if I am a dependent or even a mistress," she says swinging her feet over the counter's edge.

I must stifle an angry growl at her mention of leaving me. My temper will not help this situation, but it doesn't stop rage from clouding my vision. There is no way I am ever letting her go. My possessive streak needs a more delicate way of telling her that than with a growl. Her eyes are glassy with tears. Somewhere along the way, I have made my queen feel like she is a side project. A weight crushes into my chest as I see the pain in her eyes. I need to show her I can be sensitive to her needs and take care of her.

I grab a towel from the rack and get down on one knee before her. I begin to dry her feet and watch the tears fall onto her legs. I'm silent because, for once, the words aren't there. She vetoed anything pretty or loving I could say to her because she no longer trusts my words. She wants a show of my intentions. I leave the towel on the floor as I grab one of her lotion bottles from the counter. I fill my palm with it to find it is the origin of her citrus scent. I divide my bounty by my two hands and transfer it to her calves.

I focus my attention on her right foot as I work the lotion down to her feet. I try to be gentle as I massage her feet with circular rubbing motions. Despite my intentions, I'm rubbing her hard enough to turn her skin pink. Her feet are rough from being constantly barefoot, so maybe I have a little leeway when I'm too rough with them or at least I hope I do. I gather her toes in my palm. I squeeze and release them repeatedly to calm her muscles.

I feel her shift and look up to see her staring wide-eyed back at me. She has leaned her back against the mirror to watch my every move. If she wants entertainment, then I am prepared to provide the show. *Challenge accepted.* I repeat the foot massage on her left foot before trailing up her calves with each hand. Her legs are so soft and silky I almost forget the fact I'm doing this for her.

I collect another palmful of lotion before caressing the backs of her knees. She twitches at the contact and I smile to myself. I scratch my nails behind them and her head rocks back. Surprise! I found an erogenous zone. I liberally moisturize her knees before moving upward.

I start trailing my hands over her thighs and watch her for feedback. Ugh, she isn't responding to my touch at all. I feel the rumble in my chest escape before I can catch it. Her eyes open and for a moment, I'm trapped by her golden stare. I hold my breath as her hands cover mine to press them brutally into her skin. I'm positive I will leave marks behind if I treat her with this amount of pressure. I feel like an ogre while my inner animal glows with satisfaction at the thought of her covered with my marks. She breaks the spell by sitting up as if to leave. I place one hand over her heart and push her back against the mirror while holding her gaze captive. I slide my other hand under her ass and slide it to the edge of the counter.

Her eyes widen in alarm as she defies gravity perched on the countertop. I push her knees apart as far as they will go and press her heels onto the counter edge. The seriousness in my expression must have conveyed my desire for her to stay because she reclines into my selected position.

Using her chosen pressure, I begin to massage my way up her thighs, leaving pink swirls in my wake. I look up to her face for reassurance, but her eyes are closed, and her chest is heaving with heavy panting motion. I'm temporarily hypnotized by her hard-tipped breasts rising and falling beneath the thin T-shirt.

Slowly, I use my tongue to caress the back of each knee. I place a path of kisses traveling toward her center. When I get very little response from her, I add little nips followed by my licks to ease the sting. I drag my nails over the wet sensitive skin, and she starts to shake. *My queen likes it rough.* I don't know if I'm more shocked or delighted. I go with delighted and use the stubble on my cheeks to stimulate her further.

I'm intoxicated by her scent before I reach the junction at the top of her thighs. She wears dainty pink cotton panties which are soaked through with arousal. My inner beast wants to roar in triumph. I can win her over. I link my fingers around the material to run my knuckles over her core. I repeat the action with increasing pressure until I find her secret code. She has scrunched her eyes closed and she's biting her lip.

Rip! I tear out the crotch from her panties in one motion. Her eyes fly open in surprise and she opens her mouth to speak as she sits up. I'm rewarded with her shocked stillness. *Two can be shocked speechless,*

Baby. I use the same hand-over-heart motion to return her back against the mirror as I did before. I stare at the beauty of her laid out before me. I focus to burn the image into my brain.

"So precious," I say breathlessly before I can stop myself. Her eyes open and she looks at me quizzically.

"So beautiful," I add as she watches me.

"You think I'm beautiful?"

"Mine," I say with a nod, and she frowns. *Too bad.* I will die before anyone else gets to gaze at her like this.

I forcefully grip her thighs to hold them open. I use my tongue, teeth, and lips to pleasure her. I hear her pant roughly above me and feel her hands grip my hair. She pushes my face forward to increase the pressure. Her knees fall open and her back arches revealing even more to my ministrations. I watch the pink blush travel from her cheeks down her ribs to her navel. She has a pair of large freckles on the underside of her left breast. I either forgot they were there or never noticed. Of course, I never noticed the tantalizing dots. Only by worshiping her from below would I have a view of her most private adornments. I have lorded over her, forgetting supporting her from below is just as powerful.

I plunge my middle finger into her weeping opening and begin to pump it at a lazy pace. Her hips begin to buck involuntarily, and little whimpers escape her reluctant lips. The temperature increases in the room and I can feel her frosty adopted-nature melting. This is my fiery goddess. Now that I am addicted to her, I need to prove I deserve her.

"I need more but I don't know what," she says

breathlessly.

"Let go. You can't have control and passion. Choose."

I score her side with my nails before clasping her hands in mine. I run them over her torso until she begins to move without my help. It is either the flush of excitement or total embarrassment that darkens her cheeks from bright pink to scarlet. I continue to pump my fingers as I watch her with hungry eyes. Waiting. Does she follow my lead or end this?

Her mouth drops open with passion as she lets the sensations wash over her. I watch her posture change as she gifts her body to my care. I add my index finger to her opening and quicken my pace as I get excited watching her. She is breathing heavily and moaning with each exhale.

She begins to quake, and I snake my arm around her for security, placing my palm on her lower back. I wish to give her comfort, freedom, and love in my arms. I want her to remember it is me giving this to her. There will be no more comments about releasing me from our marriage after tonight.

"That's it, my queen. Ride me. Take what I offer," I coo to her.

I feel her walls thicken as her body prepares to orgasm. Then her legs straighten and squeeze me with super-human strength as her entire body goes taut. I release her openings when she begins to shudder with a violent release.

I bring her back down gently, whispering nonsense to her in breathy tones. I listen to her raspy breathing as she becomes coherent again. When she's still, I lift her gently to sitting upright on the counter and push her knees back together.

"I love you, Sweetheart," I whisper from my stance on the floor. Due to our hurried marriage, I don't believe I have ever knelt before her. I denied her that moment where her chosen man gets down on one knee and declares his love. I can only hope I have made up for it tonight. If not, I wish to spend the rest of my life trying.

I can feel her begin to pulse with aftershocks and I'm reluctant to lean to my sink to wash my hands. I want to bend her over the counter and fuck the hell out of her. I must control myself though. Tonight is for her. I hook my arms under her knees and shoulders to lift her.

"Wait, you can't lift me. I'm too heavy. You will drop me," she protests.

"Correction. I have never lifted you. I can do it without dropping you. I just haven't shown you. I have done a terrible job of taking care of you...until tonight," I say into her hair. I inhale her citrus fragrance and tease out the subtle scent of the gardens. It's like her magic was always there but I missed it.

I carry her to our bed easily with my shifter strength. I can even climb up on the high mattress surface with her small form still tucked into my arms. At the jostling movement, she clutches my shirt for safety. I instantly feel ten feet tall when I have never done anything to make her feel tall. I pay the bills and expect her to be grateful. *Ugh.*

I lay her onto her side and quickly strip off my work clothes, leaving them on the floor. I had come home to hang the new clothes to let some of the wrinkles fall out or even coax Alison into ironing them.

Turns out the imperfections I wear run deeper than the wrinkles on clothes. I don't care about my appearance as much now.

I curl my body around hers and reach for the bedspread to cover us. At first, she stiffens with her heartbeat thundering through the room. I lock her against me with my arm and use it to feel the slow rise of her stomach as she slowly falls asleep. I listen to her breathe in the darkness as I try to figure out how I am going to balance everything.

Chapter 18

A rumbling snore combined with the first rays of morning sunlight have my eyes snapping open in alarm. Heavy limbs pin me to the mattress. For the first time in nearly a decade, I have awoken in Grant's embrace. As tempting as it is to fall under his spell, I retreat to my garden to process last night's events.

I go through my morning routine while completely lost in my thoughts. What could have caused Grant's complete change in attitude?

He admitted he needed to treat me differently, but did he mean as a partner or something else? If his goal was to answer my questions concerning our relationship, we are in trouble. He raised more questions. The only thing that changed is my ever-increasing addiction to him. Images of him crouched at my feet cause fluttering within my most secret, and sore, parts. His admission of love is burnt into my psyche for all time. I was too stunned to return the sentiment.

Somehow, I manage to get Henrik and me to Paulino's pizzeria for class. The usually serene atmosphere of a closed restaurant is a whirlwind of chaos. Paulino boys scurry about everywhere at the command of a possessed Rosie. Stress radiates off her in pulsing waves. She looks like she's been struck by lightning with her hair standing on end and dark circles under her eyes.

At seeing my arrival, she calls to me in a frazzled voice; "Thanks again for teaching. Brad called for Frank Junior and Gran to meet him at Bergan this afternoon so I'm down two sets of hands. With the frozen tomato delivery today, I have to decant them into buckets to thaw before making the marinara for the next few weeks."

"Today is such a gray dark day my gardens will not need me. I'm always happy to help. I'll work with the little ones first so Ray and Vincenzo can help you carry, open, and dump bags. Then I'll trade you so the younger four will help to sift out whole tomatoes and take the bags out to the recycling. Does that work?" I suggest.

"Wow, you just look at a group and put them in order. You are like a chaos-eating monster. Do you want a pizzeria to run? Slightly used," Rosie says with a huge smile.

"Yeah right, I don't want your pizzeria. The first time I have to touch the dough I will go screaming for the hills!" I say with a shiver.

I look at the crates of bags and freezer packs. It looks like the supply for a mission to the South Pole. "This is a lot of work for frozen tomatoes," I say in amazement.

"I refuse to use a canned sauce. Gran's recipe is what brings all the boys to the yard," Rosie says waving her brow at me.

"I could grow this amount of tomatoes or even more in a week in my greenhouses. How attached to your frozen tomato preparation are you? I would like to apply for the job of tomato supplier," I say.

"You are the best friend I could ask for!" Rosie says while squeezing me. It was a good thing I have under-sensitive touch receptors, or I would be yelling in pain. Rosie is as short as I am but is surprisingly strong.

"Put that precious flower down!" I hear Gran yell from the doorway. She is at Frank Junior's elbow shuffling toward us. Her silvery hair is piled under a wide-brimmed hat which matches her gold-colored dress. Her knotted hands are tipped with gold-colored nail polish and her feet are adorned with golden square heels. She waves a dark wooden cane at us in menace, but her violet eyes are crinkled at the edges in laughter.

Rosie and I both groan as we are admonished. There is irony in how delicate Gran is hanging on Junior's arm while she's warning Rosie about how delicate I am. I shiver as I consider Gran as my ghost of Christmas future.

"What a beautiful hat, Gran. I love the sunflower on it. You will take Bergan by storm. They will have to resuscitate the young men in there as they faint at your feet!" I say.

"Junior is kind enough to take me to Bergan. Brad wishes for me to meet your man," Gran says.

"Mine? Grant? Whatever for?" I ask.

"Because men are narrow-sighted, Flower. Come, we need to talk before I leave. Junior, please escort me to the table by the window. Our flower here needs what little sunlight this gray sky provides," Gran says, instantly taking charge. Rosie takes the rest of the crew to the kitchen, giving my elbow a squeeze as she leaves.

"You are very kind, Gran, but I don't have a message to send to Grant. We don't talk during the day because he needs to stay focused at work. He has requested I leave him be unless the house is on fire…" I start off. I'm anxious to get back to the boys. It is ridiculous. I feel like I've been called into the principal's office.

Rosie has so much work to do and I can feel the stress radiating from the kitchen. I'm also anxious about what Gran has to say. She doesn't speak unless it is earth-shattering. I smile to myself as she reminds me of Matteo. He must get this trait from her and it warms my heart.

"He would be smarter to focus on you," Gran retorts. I laugh at that. It feels great to have my private troubles validated by someone so wise before I have even complained to her. If only she knew how often that phrase floats through my mind.

"You have magic…" Gran starts. She adds; "Don't worry I can keep a secret" when I gasp and put my hand to my throat.

"Did you see me grow something?"

"No, but I didn't need to catch you in the act. It's as plain as your face. The mark is in your eyes, Henrik's eyes, and my eyes too. We are quite a trio. A trio that is highly valued by the wrong kind of beings."

"Beings?! Now, I'm not an animal whisperer but I've never had trouble with other species."

"No dear, there are beings in this town you haven't met. Scary, twisted beings who live to get their hands on a flower like you. They raid this town on the night of the new moon so they can hide in the darkness."

"I bet that is why Grant was so adamant about having a security system even though we are surrounded by countryside. I was so confused since the statistics showed crimes are almost non-existent here."

"We are less than a week from the next new moon. Promise me you and Henrik will be careful after dark. They can't break into your house. They won't break glass or doors down to get you but don't let them in. If you hear a noise, don't go out to check on it, especially alone."

"Sounds reasonable. Who are these people? Are they a traveling motorcycle gang, crazed students from a neighboring college with a tradition of kidnapping, human traffickers?"

"More terrible than any of those. I wanted to give you this before I leave. Keep it with you whenever you are outside."

She hands me a little fabric bag with odd symbols stitched onto it. I open it gently to reveal a small vial and a larger vial. The small vial holds a clear liquid while the larger vial is full of what looks like salt crystals. "This is a beautiful bag, but I don't understand the contents," I say.

"The liquid is moon water or water that has been left out under the full moon to absorb its radiation. The crystals are a mixture of salt and mountain ash from a blessing ritual I perform under the full moon. The radiation will give you power, Henrik too. However, it is useless to anyone else."

"I love being under the full moon. Thank you so much for a pocket full of moonlight," I say. I get up to gently hug her frail frame. I have a pinch of nostalgia as this gift reminds me of the magical gifts my aunt would give to me as a child. I wonder what my life would be like if my mother were magical and wise like Gran.

"In helping you, I'm helping everyone. Don't hide inside your petals, Flower. I can feel the strength pouring off you. The men overlook you and hopefully, our enemy will too—at least until you let them have it!" She says with a clap of her hands during the last phrase. Her eyes are sparkling over her crinkled grin like she knows where there's a secret stash of chocolate. Her joy is infectious, and I return her smile as I help her up.

"Junior," she calls. "I need you to take me to Bergan now. This flower has people to organize, work to do, and magic to spread." Frank Junior comes running like he's been shot from a cannon. He takes her elbow from me and leads her out the front door.

I tuck the bag into my back pocket and stride into the kitchen. The room is a red-stained mess. Open bags of tomatoes line the countertops like members of a choir with their mouths hanging open. Five boys are sitting on the floor with their arms submerged in individual buckets of red goop.

They are fishing for tomatoes, placing each treasure in a bucket at the center of the mess. Rosie is at the stove caramelizing onions while Ray is chopping herbs at a furious pace. All the kitchen inhabitants are covered in blotches of red, giving the room a look of a massacre taking place.

"This is the last time we do this," Rosie sings as I enter. She waves her spoon at me in defiance. "You are hired as a tomato supplier. We are weighing each bucket of tomatoes so you will have an ideal weekly weight to produce. We can negotiate from there."

I'm so happy to see Rosie calm and in charge. Gone is the frazzled woman from this morning and she is replaced with the Rosie everyone loves. I start chopping herbs at Ray's side and together we quickly make neat piles of them all.

"The oregano is from our plants. We trimmed them when they got too big and had enough clippings for sauce today. Mom is calling this marinara, Fresh Oregano Red Sauce on the menu," Ray says to me quietly.

"I'm so proud of all of you. You must be taking excellent care of your plants to yield this much," I say loud enough for the boys on the floor to hear it. I'm answered with a chorus of "my bucket is empty" as each of the boys finish at that precise moment.

"Ray, take their finished tomatoes, rinse them, and weigh them. We can now give Alison a total. Boys take your buckets out back to dump them down the sewer. Then rinse them using the hoses and rinse yourself too before bringing them to the dish area. Alison, help Tommy carry his bucket, so it doesn't slosh all over the floor," Rosie says in a booming voice.

"How would you notice new sloshes?" I laugh holding the back door open, indicating the stains on the floor. Anthony leads the way outside while Vinnie and Matteo follow through my open door.

Rosie takes a tomato from Ray's bucket and hurls it at me. It squishes as it hits me right over the heart. I dip my fingers in Henrik's bucket as he passes through the door and fling tomato water at her. It splats across her face giving her tomato-scented war paint. Rosie calmly turns off the stove and places her spoon on the rest at her side. She then charges at me, grabbing Tommy's bucket along the way.

Seeing the imminent danger, I race outside and grab Henrik's bucket. I hold it in front of me as Rosie flings the entire contents of Tommy's bucket at me. I duck but still get a shower of tomato water. Now Rosie is unarmed, and I still have Henrik's bucket. The boys are laughing like hyenas as we circle each other. The three boys with buckets intact hold them close like security blankets. Rosie and I are laughing too. She playfully tries to swat Henrik's bucket out of my arms. She doesn't realize how strong I have become over the last week. My nightly yoga has made me as strong as she is.

I can see the surprise in her eyes as her swats become more aggressive. I pick a large tomato out of my hair and calmly drop it to the ground. I circle away from it and back again while dodging Rosie's moves. As if following a choreographed routine, Rosie steps on the tomato I had dropped. As she wobbles to keep her balance, I dump Henrik's bucket over her head. There is a collective gasp as her boys are stunned.

Then my traitorous son grabs a handful from Anthony's bucket and flings it at the back of my head. Rosie tackles me and we end up rolling on the ground, laughing hysterically. The remaining three buckets get dumped over us as the other boys fall prey to our fun. We separate but are too winded to stand. Being soaked to the bone causes me to feel a chill and I shiver.

Suddenly, Ray explodes out of the kitchen door. "Everyone back in. Let's go quickly, please. Anthony help Tommy, Mom help Henrik and Matteo help Alison. We can't have anyone hurt…from…slipping," he says. He gives Rosie a pointed look before saying the last phrase. I feel a knot form in my stomach as Matteo pulls me to standing.

"Yep, let's hurry back, there's work to do," Rosie says toward the sky. I'm feeling really uneasy now. Matteo all but pushes me into Ray as we shuffle through the doorway. Rosie pushes Henrik inside but steps out of the way for Tommy and Anthony to enter. The entire time she and Vinnie are scanning the sky. Could this town have a bird problem too?

Images from Hitchcock's film fill my head. Combined with my odd conversation with Gran, I picture Rosie and Vinnie fighting off giant Pterodactyls. Mosquitos have always bitten Henrik and me more than anyone else in the same vicinity; maybe it is the same for these birds. Another shiver runs through my body.

Ray gives Anthony a look over my head. Anthony has put Tommy into the dishwashing sink to hose him down with the sprayer. "Alison, Henrik, do you guys want to rinse off over here? I got the water hot," Anthony says to us.

"You are shivering. That will help you warm up," Ray says all but pushing us away from the door and toward the sink. Ray stays by the door watching the sky as the others come in to join us.

The boys must wash the tomato juice out of their clothes, or they will create a trail of red stains through the dining room and up to their apartment. Dripping soap is better than dripping red pulp and seeds. Soon everyone is lathering, scrubbing, and rinsing. Everyone seems normal and joking around like all that weirdness coming inside didn't happen. Rosie announces Junior has Gran inside Bergan and everyone looks relieved for some reason. Is Gran a bird magnet too?

Henrik shoots me a quizzical look. He's daring me to ask about all this. I give my head a little shake. It's not our business why it is so important that Gran is at Bergan. However, that's not going to stop me from asking Gran about the birds the next time she wants to chat about mystic matters.

Chapter 19

I'm back at my desk with a new task list ready for my attention. Too bad my attention is still in the gardens behind my house. I have one item written: *Ask Brad to explain enemies' weaknesses.* That's a lynchpin to all this so as soon as I get my feet moving, I will track down Brad.

My mind wanders back to my wife. When I woke up this morning, I found all my new clothes ironed and hanging up. I found coffee made and Henrik waiting with breakfast at the table. Henrik explained Alison was back in the garden gathering more basil to take to Rosie today.

I had an excellent breakfast of bagels and lox, fruit salad and tuna tartar on toast. What made breakfast even better is I got over an hour of Henrik joyfully telling me about how he spends his days. It had been too long since I checked in with him. I was grateful he opened up, forgiving me for being away. *I have a great kid.* I sigh to myself.

I reach for more dried cranberries and find I emptied my bag. I wonder if Alison would want to grow cranberries. Do they grow on bushes, trees or vines? No, they grow in bogs. I will build a giant cranberry bog for her. If she wants one, not for my cranberry habit but so she sees I consider her a partner. An accomplice or supplier to my cranberry addiction.

This is the perfect metaphor for where we are now, just I am completely driven to distraction by her like an addict.

"Earth to Grant! Earth to Grant! This is Earth are you hearing us, Grant?" I hear a voice from over my shoulder. The hand waving in front of my face is about to be broken. I swat at it and turn to face its owner. Nate stands behind my desk with a smirk on his face.

"Aaaaaaannnnnnnnnnnd he's back. Good morning, Sunshine. I thought you had been abducted by aliens and replaced by a pod person for a bit there," Nate says.

"Sorry, I'm a little distracted this morning," I say in a groggy voice.

"Well, get in the game. We are meeting Brad in five minutes in his office. James is already on his way there, but I thought I would get you to hunt for donuts with me," Nate says.

"Huh?" That's all I can get out. I was going to schedule a meeting that was already scheduled. A double-booked redundant meeting. A super meeting. This is not like me. I'm horrified. I need to snap out of it.

"Guess your email silence means you didn't read the ones we were sending. James assumed it was because you were being a geezer and drawing on your board. Now I'm really glad I came to get you," Nate says getting right in my face.

I push him away, gather my meeting supplies, and head for the door. Nate takes a photo of my board with his phone as if I wrote it this morning. The old notes are my only saving grace. I will hide behind them so they can't see how lost I feel. I need information to finish my plan and I need to get a grip to get it.

When I walk into Brad's office, he is on the phone. "Just visitor badges and send them up," he says before hanging up. Nate and I join James sitting at the conference at the opposite end of the room.

"I need a list of the Sluagh's weaknesses, their current numbers, and a blueprint of their fortress. How much documentation do we have on them? Is there an electronic file I can download or do I need to retrieve something from the file room?" I start.

"We have none of that," says James with a smirk.

"None of what? Electronic copies?" I ask.

"Frankie wasn't too big on documentation. He was more a man of action. That's why I have called in our expert to tell you firsthand our history with the Sluagh," says Brad.

"Can't they send it in an email? I assume this expert is on the Bergan payroll.".

"Negatory on both," Nate quips.

"How can we have an expert in town but not at Bergan?"

"Because some of us need to breathe; we are smart enough not to get caught in concrete traps baited with money," says a feminine voice from the doorway. I recognize Frank Junior at the door holding his grandmother's elbow to lead her in.

I look incredulously at Brad. No wonder I had no hope of getting an email, zipped file or attachment from the expert. I'm still gaping at them when all the men at the table stand in respect.

"Rafaella, you look like a beam of sunshine. Come in and meet Grant," says Brad getting up to welcome her. He embraces her lightly and pulls his desk chair to the conference table. He offers it to her, and she sits gently like a monarch. I take her hand lightly in greeting but she squeezes my hand until my knuckles crack.

She is stronger than she looks, and she has no scent. She's a loophole in the "all females stink" side effect. She is an amazing anomaly for that alone. If I could learn what she uses to mask her scent, then I could spread it around the office. The shifter smell experience holds back our company from optimal efficiency. Brad and Frank Junior take conference chairs on either side of her.

"Thank you as always, Brad. Now everyone calls me Gran, though. I'm as old as time," Gran blushes.

"We know better than that," says James warmly.

"I still remember when I came here with Molina. You were so kind to us, Molina especially. I introduced you to Vincenzo the morning we snuck into his barn to sleep. He was quite taken with you. It was the only thing that kept him from eating us," Brad reminisces.

"Your young guns look thoroughly confused," Gran says with a twinkle in her eyes. She nods in my direction.

"Born shifters and blood exchange shifters age about eight times slower than humans. We live to be around eight hundred years old. Rafaella, sorry Gran, started to age at human speed when we lost her mate, Vincenzo. Vincenzo was the leader before their son, Frankie. They suffered the same fate," Brad explains.

"Wait, now I have more questions than answers. What happened to Frankie and Vincenzo? Do leaders live shorter lives than humans?"

Gran turns to me and looks me right in the eye. It's a powerful stare but her eyes are strangely familiar, causing her to be less intimidating. "Leaders and their mates have a long lifespan except they tend to be brave and stand at the front in the battles. Leaders and their mates can partially shift but otherwise are identical to other shifters. I'm aging because my life as a shifter was directly tied to Vincenzo but not by a blood exchange," Gran says, wiggling her eyebrows at the end.

"For that to work, you would have to be a..." I stammer in amazement.

"Yes dear, I'm a witch. I was born a witch; my children and children's children have Wiccan blood in various amounts. None of them have the mark of a witch or the powers, but maybe the next generation will. Who knows?" Gran says, shrugging her shoulders.

"We thought you would be the best person to counsel Grant on the Sluagh. We are about thirty hours from the new moon. Grant needs to put a plan in place in the event of an attack," Brad says.

"There will be an attack. No doubt. I got a text from Mom saying they had a fly-over at the pizzeria. No one was snatched but she wants to make sure Gran is safe inside. I'm replying we are secure in here," Frank Junior says.

"Wow, very cunning of them to go after the one person who can diagram their strategies. Even more reason to get their information into a written format. Let's start with a 360 review of their approach," I say. When all I get is a stare in return I add, "Sensory clues as to their arrival...as in how they smell, what they look like, the sounds they make, you know."

"Or I will tell you their story and you can learn it, chart it, write it, tell it or whatever you want with it. I refuse to dissect what I have lived in fear of my whole life. They aren't just bad neighbors; they are outcasts for the most heinous of crimes," Gran says in a flat voice.

I start to talk but Nate squeezes my arm. I'm receiving glares from every set of eyes at the table. I feel slighted as their leader when it's obvious Gran is calling the shots. I don't have time for storytelling. I add *Google Sluagh mythology* to my task list.

"My Vincenzo caught one when Frankie was a teen. The Sluagh was an ugly creature. Gray leathery skin barely hanging onto his bony frame. A few long strings of hair were loyal to his scalp when all the others had left. He had no color to his eyes—not even white—just black pits framed by gray lashes. His lips must have been taken by the Fae too for all he had was a gaping hole full of pointy teeth. His teeth weren't even impressive, tiny triangles rooted in black gums. His claws were much more formidable especially since the ones on his hands matched the ones on his feet," Gran starts.

"Sounds like an Adonis," I quip.

"He was a miserable, pitiful creature. The Fae live and die by their looks, so his appearance was a part of his punishment. The Sluagh are former fairies who have been cast out of the Fae for bad behavior. I'm not sure of their due process procedures but our hostage told us how he got here.

"The Fae are a vain race who love the pleasures of the flesh. However, they have strict boundaries that cannot be crossed. No giving others pain to make yourself feel good. Every act and pairing must be between mutually consenting adult fairies. No fairy owns, sells or buys time with another fairy.

"Everyone there is beautiful to blinding perfection, but he was humiliated by being reduced to that form AND THEN cast here. They taunt him with names like The Under Folk, The Host of the Unforgiven and The Wilds on the way out. He did have one redeeming feature. Funny, he was most ashamed of his beautiful wings. I guess all the Fae have glass-like wings that develop colors with each depraved act," Gran says with tears in her eyes.

"Nosferatu with butterfly wings, got it," I say looking at my notes. I doodle a butterfly in the corner.

Gran doesn't continue until I look up at her. As she tries to bore holes into my skull with her eyes, I study them. They are bright violet with silver near the pupil. I can't remember anyone with violet eyes so I can't explain the nagging feeling of déjà vu.

"A cold chill always precedes them," Nate says to break the silence.

"The cold comes from their diet of sadness and hopelessness. You risk getting a fly-over whenever someone is nursing a broken heart. That is why you must never torture, allow a slow death, or even detain the enemy for long periods of time. We found this out the hard way. I spent lots of time sitting with the miserable creature to get information for my Vincenzo but also to ease his suffering. Suffering calls to them like a lighthouse in the fog. The same goes for your pack, your family, and yourself. You must take care of their hearts as well as keep them safe," Gran warns me.

That explains the fly-over at my house after my turn. Alison must have been broadcasting our problems over the Sluagh emotional superhighway. I put on my list to talk to her about that and circle it. Gran watches

149

me doodle and reads it upside-down. I get a disapproving frown. "Why set up here? Why not park next to a hospital and feast away?" I ask to keep the conversation going.

"The Sluagh could do that but the one we caught wasn't trying to survive here. He was frantic to be beautiful again. If they get ahold of a shifter heart, a double soul, they get temporary Fae glamor. He was trying to get back to the Fae, permanently. For that, they need a new triple soul," Gran answers in a matter-of-fact tone. I shoot Brad a look and he's nodding in agreement.

"How does a Sluagh extract a soul? What is their procedure to get back to the Fae?" I ask, trying desperately to understand.

"By the time our hostage got to that part, it was time to put him down. The others of his flock were circling, and the battle had arrived at our doorstep," Gran says in a huff.

"The battle? You never mentioned a battle. What are their tactics, weapons, weaknesses, fighting formations?" I ask with eagerness.

"You had me skip that part of the story with your questions. You aren't a good listener," she replies primly.

My jaw drops and my eyes bug out. Is she really withholding life-saving information to teach me about listening like an errant kindergartener? I glare at Brad who has the audacity to be snickering with James. I can't believe this. This pack needs a good dose of professionalism and organization.

"Rafaella, please..." starts Brad in my defense, as if I need a defense.

She starts to gather her purse and cane, saying, "Brad, I promised my Vinnie on his deathbed I would use my premonitions to aid the pack leader. I have talked to the leader today, so my conscience is clear. We will survive the next battle because the Sluagh numbers are small in the fortress. I can't hear many voices wailing in the night." As she stands everyone else stands in respect for her.

"I appreciate your wisdom and willingness to share it with us. It is always a pleasure to see you," Brad says.

"With my Vinnie gone, this pack has been my focus. I feel it is in good hands now. A few lessons need to be learned then I will feel ready to join my love," she says smiling to Brad.

"Rafaella, you don't mean that," James blurts out.

"Almost, my dear. I miss my Vinnie too much. I feel his touch in the sunlight, hear his voice in rainstorms, and taste his kiss in the air I breathe. Once you hold true love in your hands, it is hard to live without it. I don't wish this on anyone," she says in my direction. James reaches for her hand and pats it gently. They exchange sad smiles as if sharing a secret.

I'm even more lost than before. I had no idea she could tell the future, hear the enemy, or identify how many of them we were facing. I wished she hadn't wasted the meeting by telling a story. I chastise myself for not setting an itemized agenda while I was staring into space at my desk. The only reprieve I give myself is there was no way I would have guessed my meeting was going to be crashed by a psychic witch, who was a stickler for good listening.

As the door closes with the visitors on the other side, I turn the page in my notes to a clean sheet. "Now let's get to business. Since we have battled them before, we must have an arsenal hidden at Bergan. How much are we talking in handhelds, vehicles, large artillery?"

"Zero," James says with a snicker.

"Bullets and heavy projectiles go right through the Sluagh as if they are shadows," explains Brad.

"Shadows? So, do we shoot them with lasers?" I ask incredulously.

"Slow down, Space Commander. The Fae need to be ripped to pieces and buried upside down to be killed," Nate says.

"What?" I say with my eyes bulging.

"If a Sluagh is ripped to pieces, they can use the energy from the sun to knit themselves back together. So, Frankie had the procedure of dismembering and pile. At the end of the battle, we would dig a pit about ten to fifteen feet deep. We would put the heads in first, a foot of dirt, wings, foot of dirt, torso with claws, foot of dirt, and so on. At the top, we would pile rocks to keep anything reassembled from rising," Brad clarifies.

"So, if they are shadows, then how are they cut to pieces? Does Bergan's arsenal include a bunch of bulldozers for all the digging?" I ask, while my mind flies a mile per minute.

"I carry iron sai. Josh's friend Josh is a master blacksmith. He makes iron weaponry at the auto shop. He can make anything you want to cut the Sluagh. That's why he's on Bergan's payroll instead of Josh's," James says, pulling out wicked mini-tridents from his holster. They are only about ten inches long but heavy when I pick one up. I'm in awe of the craftsmanship. There are little symbols engraved into it. The runes are so clear they must have been drawn with a laser.

"The symbols are an incantation. Rafaella wrote it for me," James adds with a glare in my direction.

"However, most of us shift and use claws in battle. Those claws are also efficient at digging. So yeah, Bergan is housing a large arsenal, but you would call it our personnel," Nate retorts.

"Hence, the sweat suits..." I surmise.

"Frankie put non-clawed members in charge of coming back here during the digging. They were to change and bring clothes for the rest of us who weren't close to their home," Brad says.

"If Frankie had all these procedures, where are they written? Why wasn't I given a "what Frankie does" manual when I showed you my partial shift?"

"That wasn't Frankie's way. He was more about people than paper," James says quietly.

"He would have town meetings and get everyone involved. Paulino's isn't open every night because we use it as a headquarters. Rosie could be making more money, but she respects that the space is valuable because Gran maintains wards around the building. It has been our meeting place before Bergan was even a thought," Brad says.

"He let everyone in on our secret? Is that how he kept everyone safe?"

"We invented reasons to warn people outside of the shifters to stay indoors during the New Moon. We posted fake mosquito spraying signs, spread rumors of impending snowstorms, and closed roads for imaginary night paving. The Sluagh will not break into a home. They will fly into open windows or doors though. Vents are too small. We watch their homes if we think they may be of interest to the Sluagh. If they get a fly-over, the person has a few options for survival if they don't freeze with fright.

"They could outrun the Sluagh to a sunny spot at dawn or dusk, they could hide in a space too deep and small for the Sluagh's reach, or they could try to fight it. Sadly, most civilians end up getting their heart eaten so the Sluagh can enjoy temporary glamor," Brad says.

"Speaking of glamor. Have you had a full shift yet? Do you know what you are working with?" James asks.

"I thought it was rude to ask," I reply with a smirk. "I haven't had the strength to fully shift. I'm big, slow, and have mean claws."

"You need to practice so you can shift quickly and stay in animal form during the battle. The effects of shifting back to human form will temporarily incapacitate you. That's not how you want to be in battle," Brad says.

"Well, there's no time like the present," James says challengingly, shutting the blinds.

I see red. *How dare he?* I slip off my shoes with malice and prepare to shift. My anger fuels the shift, so I swiftly change forms. It's so fast I barely feel the hairs sprout or my bones change shape. I growl in James's direction and take in their shocked faces.

Chapter 20

"What a day," I say aloud to my empty house. I've been hunched over the kitchen counter making bundles of herb blends to be dried. Strung around the kitchen like Christmas lights, bundles of Italian blends, poultry seasonings, bedtime teas, and dessert flavorings fill the house with their wild fragrances. Gazing at my handiwork, I reach up to hear my shoulders pop.

Rolling them back yields more creaking protests. I need to stretch before going to bed or I will wake up sore tomorrow. I look out my giant windows to see a sliver of the moon traveling across the sky. That's enough to scare away Gran's evil birds, right? I grab the gift she gave me off the kitchen counter and head outside.

How inconvenient. My leggings and sweatshirt have no pockets. When will they start making women's clothing with pockets a standard? Once outside, I place the bag in my gardening apron to free my hands. It feels colder than it has been the last few nights, as the wind picks up. There are fewer insect sounds each passing night as winter slowly approaches. However, it still smells like fall. The leaves are damp and molding on the ground like a brown carpet laid out for the impending arrival of a snow queen.

I climb up on the balcony railing, wide enough to be a bench really, to get the rush of being two stories above the ground. I lay on my back to take in my surroundings. Leaves dance in the wind, giving the night a magical feel and I feel grateful to be in its audience. I look carefully for whatever flying thing had spooked Rosie and the kids this morning.

Their reaction was so strange, but I guess this town has a major vulture problem. I relax when I can see no vultures in my field of view unless you count my creepy neighbor with the binoculars. I flash my middle finger at him, and he has the audacity to wave his hand over his head. *Creeper.*

When he shows no sign of moving, I decide to forget him. He's not going to see anything he hasn't watched nightly for the last two weeks. *Outrageous creeper.* I flip over and raise my torso off the railing. I breathe in the night air, close my eyes and listen.

I can hear rustling under the trees beyond my gardens as the night creatures forage for food. I put extra seedlings at the edge of my space to provide food for them, hoping they will not venture farther to damage my hoop houses. I make a mental note to find some windows to repurpose into cold boxes for the lower beds.

I lower my torso back to the railing and sigh happily. I love the night. There isn't as much moonlight as I would like, but I love the peaceful rhythmic sounds. I take a deep breath in and hoist my hips into the air. I adjust my feet until the tendons stretch to the point of tingling. Then I slowly lean my weight toward my hips to pull on my shoulders.

Oh, how I love the slow releasing of those tight muscles. I feel the gentle liberation of all the tension built up within the day's work. My spine lengthens as my arm muscles become more forgiving. I pause with my eyes closed and breathe.

"Grrrrrrrrrrrrrrrrrrrrrrrrrrrr." I hear an ominous growling sound from behind one of my hoop houses. It is directed away from me, but it is still close enough to raise the hair on my arms. I instantly collapse off the railing onto the deck floor. My heart is pounding. I scan the skies. Once. Twice. I don't see anything up there. Thrice. My heart rate begins to slow. It's not the raptors. It's below me.

I look to my ogling neighbor as the noise was directed his way. He has put his binoculars down and is heading back inside. So, I'm good enough to spy on but not good enough to warn of incoming danger? Good thing I'm not dependent on him for a rescue. Being alone so often, I can protect myself.

Fueled by my inner fire at being interrupted, I launch myself over the railing and down to the yard below. I land in a crouch but stand to full height to survey my land. I may look small, but my gardens are my territory. "Who is out there?" I call into the darkness.

There are shuffling and chuffing noises coming from behind the hoop house to my left. I turn to it so I can face my trespasser head-on. "Show yourself, coward. You brought this on yourself by coming here. One more time: Who. Is. Out. There?" I project in my most fierce teacher-voice. I walk right up to the hoop house to peer through the Tyvek material. I see a giant hill. Did this intruder come over on horseback?

Slowly, a palatial brown bear trundles out from behind the hoop house. My body weighs my options: fight, flight, freeze, or faint. My brain and body agree to freeze. The animal isn't charging me, baring his teeth or clawing at the ground. I sense no aggression as I study him but rather something else. He's breathtakingly beautiful. Lethal black claws tip giant round paws. He's the size of my VW Beetle but covered with a thick brown coat.

He looks so soft my hands tingle to run my fingers over his coat, like an idiot. I continue to study his face to find puffs of hot breath creating smoky clouds at the end of his muzzle. It is full of pointy teeth, rimmed with pouty black lips ending in a large black nose.

I shiver and fold my arms around my waist. The action plunges the neckline of my shirt forward, flashing cleavage at the bear. As I adjust my top, I see a round pink tongue leave the bear's mouth to caress its lips. Shit, I moved so now I'm appetizing. I slowly bend down to reach inside the hoop house. I pull out a small pumpkin and break it at the stem. I whisper a thank you for saving me to the vine and offer the pumpkin to the bear. "Let me live. I gift this to you if you will let me live. Actually, take all the produce. Just let me live," I say, setting the pumpkin between us.

The bear chuffs and steps over the pumpkin. My muscles finally start cooperating and I walk backward. I regress three steps when I trip over a rut in the yard. I feel myself falling and twist around to reach out to catch myself. I grip fur. The bear has lunged out to catch me and now I'm leaning on it completely. So much for running for my life. *I'm totally bear food now.* The bear turns his face toward me. I'm struck by bright blue eyes framed with dark lashes.

They look just like Grant's eyes and I'm instantly swamped with guilt. I'm leaving Grant to raise Henrik alone because I was dumb enough to ignore his warnings and be eaten by a bear. My last hope is the bear will be moved by my tears enough to just trash my gardens and not eat me. I release the bear's fur from my clutches to curl into a ball on the ground.

"Alison, please don't cry. It's me," says the bear. Funny that I haven't felt his bite but I'm already hallucinating from loss of blood. I squeeze my eyes shut with dread.

"Alison, you are safe with me. If anything, I'm afraid of you and your power over me," says the bear in a voice eerily similar to my husband's voice.

I take inventory over my limbs, fingers, and toes. Are there talking bears in the afterlife? There are no pains or missing pieces, so I guess I haven't been eaten yet. I boldly open my eyes to find I'm nose to snout with the bear. I scream and the bear doesn't even flinch. I watch the bear lift a giant claw and raise it slowly toward my face. I brace for impact. *Please just kill me quickly*. I watch the claw morph into a human hand. The hand caresses my face as I scream again.

"Alison, please let me explain. It is so weird, but I can't keep this from you. I need you to understand. I need you on my side. I just…need…you," says the bear. I stare into his blue eyes and I see dejection, sadness, and isolation. Now that the fear has subsided, I feel empathy toward the bear. It is not easy being alone.

"OK, as long as you are not hungry, we can talk. I guess. If this is a big hallucination, I can roll with it," I say in a shaky voice while sitting up to face the bear.

"You aren't hallucinating or losing your mind. I was changed into a shape-shifter a few days or weeks ago. Time has flown so fast. I can no longer pinpoint where my crazy journey has begun. You must believe I'm me. I'm Grant," says the bear.

I study his eyes which do look exactly like Grant's eyes. The bear's muzzle shrinks into Grant's nose and mouth. I recognize his high cheekbones and the aristocratic angles to his face. Standing next to me is my husband with a human face and a bear's body. My vision begins to spin, and I feel I may pass out. I cover my eyes with my hands to block out what I can never un-see. *Nope still there.* At least he's back to all bear when I open my eyes again.

"Look, I came tonight to watch you. I wasn't planning on showing you this. I never meant to scare you. I couldn't contain the change when I saw our neighbor was watching you too. I hope my growling scared him off."

"I think you were successful. Who needs a knight in shining armor when you have a grizzly bear?" I say, laughing a little at my situation. Oh well, my friend has a witch for a mother-in-law so maybe it's not so strange to be married to a bear in this town.

"Hey, I'm not one hundred percent bear. I can go back to my human form."

"Then will you do that? I'm not comfortable enough having this conversation with this version of you. I still have an in-grown fear of being eaten by a bear."

"The last time I ate you, there was a lot of screaming but I don't believe you were in pain."

"Yeah, too odd. Rule number one: no flirting when in the bear form."

"How about rule number one: always be cognizant of who is outside with you at night. You could have been killed or worse."

"Worse than death? A little dramatic, isn't it?"

"You are talking to a bear. Let's go inside and I will turn to my human form again. I have a lot to tell you."

"You mean about the vultures? I got an earful from Rosie and Gran today. I need you to rub your bear scent all over the garden to keep them away."

"Vultures? Is that what they told you? Pffft. My bear scent won't do a thing. In fact, the longer we are out here, the more likely we are to attract them," Grant says while climbing up the stairs to our balcony. I climb up after him and smile to myself as I watch him leave claw marks on the wooden stairs. *So strange but so cool.* I open the door and let us both in, locking up tightly.

"Be sure to engage the security system because I'm going to be vulnerable for a while. When I turn back, I'm going to be passed out, maybe seizing a little, probably sweating with fever. Please don't call an ambulance. It's normal. I've been practicing so I shift quickly but there's nothing I can do during recovery," Grant says in bear form.

I watch as his snout recedes and his ears lower. His body loses mass at an alarming rate. His paws lengthen into hands and feet. His claws and fur are the last to change to nails and smooth skin. Left in the spot the bear once occupied, is my husband. He's naked, shivering and covered with twitching muscles. I remember his warning and take a deep breath to calm my panic. I use the kitchen sink to wet a washcloth with warm water and press some lavender in its folds from the hanging bundles.

I sit beside him and press the washcloth over his eyes. I shift his head into my lap to cradle it as he continues to shake. Gently I run my fingers through his hair in what I hope is a soothing motion. I'm rewarded when he winds his arms around my waist. We sit together as the shivers become slower and slower. I risk jostling him to reach for a blanket slung haphazardly over the couch. I fling it over his form and hold us still until I see him open his eyes.

"Welcome back," I whisper while smiling down at him.

"It feels good to be home," he whispers back. My breath hitches as he raises his head. I allow his lips to brush across mine before breaking the contact.

"I'm going to need more explanation than this," I whisper with tears in my eyes.

Chapter 21

He ~~lays~~ in my lap for so long I start to think that he's not going to tell me anything. Then it all comes tumbling out. He tells me about the night of his car accident and how Nate, the snow leopard shifter, caused it. He explains how James infected him with the shifter parasite and how it was all ordered by Brad. He details the hopes of Bergan that he would be an alpha shifter. He tells me that being able to shift one body part at a time is the mark of the alpha shifters as well as their mates.

"So, let me get this straight. You have worms that make you turn into a bear thanks to James?" I ask while raising an eyebrow at him. Perhaps it was best he shifted before explaining because there is no way I would have believed this wild tale otherwise.

"He did give me a parasite, but he didn't make me a bear. The parasite magnifies whatever animal is at the base of your soul. They were all hoping for a predator like a big cat or a wolf. I am a bear," Grant says with a shrug.

"I could have told them you are a grouchy bear," I snap. Unbelievable. I rub my eyes in frustration.

"I deserve that I guess. My baser personality has been magnified ever since the infection and I'm insulting people left and right. The worst is knowing I have hurt you."

"We have a decade of practice hurting each other which we can't blame on a parasite. In fact, you have been quite...quite...amorous since the accident. Are you attributing your behavior to the parasite too?"

"The parasite magnifies my baser self but doesn't create the feelings I have for you. I may have acted less civilized than before the transition, but the desire has always been there."

"The last time we were alone you said you loved me."

"Yes, Alison—"

"—I love you too, Grant. I always have. I never stopped when we weren't getting along. I should have said it sooner."

"At the risk of ruining our reconciliation, I must ask—"

"Ask what?"

"How long have you been hiding your magic growing powers from me?"

His stare has an intensity I cannot face, so I drop my gaze in submission. This is not going to go well. Pushing my fears of rejection aside, I take a leap of faith. My honest admission calls tears to the corners of my eyes but I can't help it.

"I was born with the ability to grow plants by touching them. I was raised to hide it. I have struggled my entire life to fit in and have been teased as long as I can remember for my disorder. Do you think I wanted to draw attention to my magical green thumb?"

"But you hid it from me?"

"How could I trust you? It has felt like you had one foot out the door since we got married," I say with tears rolling down my face. I wait for him to deny it, rage at me or fall into another of the toxic behaviors from our past.

"Can we build that trust now?"

I nod vigorously because I am at a loss for words. This is the fresh start I have been waiting for since we moved. No more analysis. Even if he reverts to his old habits, I have tonight. A night where I can open all my secrets to him and be accepted, even loved, for who I am and not who I pretend to be.

"So I want to hear it from you," he says, cupping his hands around my jaw. "Do you have any other magical powers like spell casting, precognition or sorcery?"

"No," I say, beaming down at him, "I have no other abilities. I garden with magic. That's it. I promise I hide no more secrets. You have all of me now."

"I'm honored, Love. I'm sorry. We have wasted so many years" he says, leaning upward to kiss me.

"Wait," I say pushing his shoulders down. "You aren't going to turn me into a shifter, are you?"

"I asked about it, but James said if I do a blood exchange it will not work. It only worked for him because he is born a shifter. I asked him to change you, but we agreed it wouldn't be helpful since your inner power is probably not predatory. This is all to aid the town against the enemy. Alison, we are at war."

Part of me feels relieved I didn't have to keep Grant at arm's length while the other part of me is furious that I am slighted again. He and his friend agree I am too weak to participate in their wargames. I guess I should be used to him seeing me as damaged, but it still hurts. "At war with the vultures, right?" I ask in a shaky voice.

Grant tells me the story of his strange meeting with Brad, Nate, James, Frank Junior, and Gran. I keep quiet and try to focus on what he is saying. It is all too much. My head is starting to spin. I am living in a horror movie and I am not a scream queen kind of girl. I stood my ground against a bear.

I even negotiated with it before retreating and falling over. Why wasn't I getting any credit for not being paralyzed with fear or screaming with hysterics during any of this?

"Hmmm, Gran is a witch…that explains so much," I say when he finishes.

"What do you mean?" Grant asks.

"She cornered me at Paulino's. I guess she was trying to warn me of the Sluagh without anyone else knowing what she was doing. She was speaking in a weird code while I was doing a lot of smiling and nodding. She gave me a little bag of vials. Now, where did I put it?" I say, shifting to look around where I'm sitting.

"Oh rats, I must have left it outside," I say, getting up and moving toward the door. Grant shoots to his feet and grabs my wrist before I can touch the lock. I look at his hand on my wrist and follow it up his arm. The new curves and hollows created by his defined bicep muscles are mouth-watering. As I turn toward him, I take in his wide shoulders, broad chest, and a much larger frame than I remember.

More planes and valleys from miles of muscles cover his torso and abdomen. He still isn't wearing clothes and I feel my breathing accelerate. He's bigger, wider and it's not just in his shoulders.

"Please, promise me you are in for the night. Do

not go outside again until the new moon is over. Let me take care of you, in here, tonight," he says to my lips.

"How about we take care of each other?" I use my free hand to grab the back of his neck and pull his lips to mine. I lick the seam of his mouth until it opens to me. Our tongues dance as I tip his head to the side and open our mouths wider to get better access. My body leans into his pressing my soft curves to his hard planes. We fit like two puzzle pieces and my heart soars. He is meant for me. The real me.

I concoct a plan to show him I am made for him too. I pull back abruptly and utilize the fact his hand is still on my wrist to pull him toward the stairs. We sneak into the bedroom like a pair of teenagers. I stop to lock the door and pull my shirt over my head. Grant watches as it falls to the floor with wide eyes.

"Alison, look about last time, I...we...I..." he stutters.

I place my hand over his mouth to stop him. "Just touch me. Don't ask. Don't hesitate. Just touch me." Not waiting to be told again, his hands rise to cup my breasts. His fingers gently whisper over my flesh as if I were made of glass. I forcibly press his hands into me and stare into his eyes.

"I'm not delicate. In fact, I'm under-sensitive to touch, remember? Even if you could hurt me, I wouldn't feel the pain." *Is that husky voice mine?* His answering smile tells me he gets the message. I see stars as his fingers begin to tease, rub and roll my pebbled flesh. My hands travel along his arms to caress his shoulders. I take his mouth again as he starts to moan, drinking the sound.

My legs go weak as the pleasure builds an inferno

inside of me. I begin to lean into him, so I don't fall over. His hands smooth downward to my waist and grip me tightly. I kick my legs out and wrap them around his waist. We align perfectly on contact. Hard ridges grind into soft valleys. We moan in unison. He carries me over to the bed and lays me onto my back.

My leggings hit the floor before I stop bouncing on the bed. He pulls my knees upward, so my feet are wide apart upon the bed. He pushes my shoulders down roughly and drags his hands over my breasts. He loops his fingers in the strings of my thong and rips it off. My torso lifts off the bed involuntarily in excitement.

"Mine," he says. His eyes are glazed with lust.

The word pulls me out of my lust-fueled haze. I sit up and place my hand over his heart. Looking him directly in the eyes, I say, "Mine".

A muscle in his jaw ticks in irritation. He places a hand over my heart only to use it to push me back down on the bed. I use my feet as leverage and scoot to the opposite side. The change in my position puts only my feet in his reach. I give him a coy smile. He roughly plants a knee on the bed and lifts himself up until he's looming over me. I shiver as I see the predator in his eyes. Too bad I'm not the prey he thinks I am.

I use my feet to squeeze at his hips. I shift my weight abruptly to the left, causing him to fall on his right side. I continue the motion until I'm positioned over him. I push his shoulder to the bed resulting in his turning onto his back. I brace him by placing each knee outside of his thighs and each foot between them. My lower legs immobilize him from the waist down. I use my weight to hold down his arms at the elbows. We lay still in the darkness, panting and staring at each other.

"I'm not the delicate flower to be left in a greenhouse alone all the time, only to be taken out to be admired when you feel like it. I'm more like the dandelion growing between the sidewalk cracks. I look small and sweet despite the inhospitable conditions. It is only because of my strength that you enjoy my softness. I choose to be docile. Do not mistake that for my only option," I hiss with fire in my eyes.

He lays there with wild eyes during my admission. I remove my hands from his elbows to maneuver his length into my wanting body. I throw my head back with an animalistic groan. He reaches up to cup my chin and bring my head down. He looks into my eyes and says, "My equal, my queen, mine." We exchange small smiles until I start to rock my hips.

I move slowly at first and then quicken as the friction builds the tension between us. He reaches up to tug my nipples into his mouth as my breasts swing over his face. My orgasm starts there and travels down until my entire body is pulsing with pleasure.

I'm vaguely conscious of his movements to adjust our position. Physically I'm returned to the position where my back is on the bed but emotionally, I'm flying around the ceiling. I feel his acceptance of my declaration to him. We are tying our hearts together as partners. He places his hands on the backs of my thighs to push them over my head. He crosses my ankles and secures them with one hand.

The other hand brushes over my nipple and I let out a small whimper. Little sparks of electricity dance over my skin. His hand continues to travel down my body until I begin to writhe. *Is that me whispering "please"?*

"I neglected you, I know, but it stops now. I promise to listen if you are telling me you are locked in a greenhouse. You have shown your petals, my Venus, fly trap, and I will never mistake you for a weaker flower ever again. Watch how your trap ensnares me," he says.

He releases my ankles and I curl into a tighter ball to watch him slowly penetrate me. I'm captivated by the erotic sight of his body entering mine, which detonates another orgasm. I begin to pulse around him. He loses control, falling over me and folding me completely in half.

Each orgasm blends into the next as he pounds relentlessly into my body. My muscles alternate between being completely unyielding and liquid as I totally lose control. I feel his body go rigid before he pours into me. He collapses and the world seems to freeze. We lay there breathing heavily in the darkness. Then he leans to whisper into my ear: "Mine".

I black out with exhaustion until the sunlight is blasting through the windows. I curse myself for not closing the curtains before falling asleep until the events of the previous night come back into focus. I contemplate whether I was dreaming or if it all really happened. The warm body coiled around my back tells me everything was real.

"Good morning," he whispers in my ear.

"I'm glad you are still here," I whisper back.

"Somehow, I lost the motivation to leave. I am distracted by the many games to be played here," he says, nibbling on my ear. As his hands travel along my body, I think to myself, this is what happiness feels like. Then my happy thoughts are popped like soap bubbles. It is the day of the new moon. Can I really keep him here when the town is depending on him?

Chapter 22

I have a spring in my step as I walk into work, two hours later than normal. The scent of fresh homemade coffee from my travel mug can't cover the citrus scent that clings to my skin and clothes. My wife drove me to work where we made out in the parking lot like teenagers. It had been a perfect morning reconnecting with my queen.

I watched her get ready for the day from our bed and learned my favorite scent is a fruit called bergamot. She rubs the oil on her wrists like perfume. She says it makes her cheerful. After having it rubbed all over me, I feel pretty damn cheerful too.

I sat with my little family and discussed what they do while I'm at work over salmon cakes. With twinkling eyes, my pair of troublemakers told me stories of tomato sauce wrestling in the streets, creepy purple flowers popping up everywhere—which I learned are called Bella Donna—and other adventures they have had in Strawberry.

Henrik kept looking from parent to parent as if he couldn't believe his eyes. Guilt pierced my heart with the realization of how much our estrangement affected him. We had stayed together for him, but we weren't truly together making our arrangement ineffective. Maybe, instead, we had stayed together to grow into what we have now. My thoughts bring a warm glow to the center of my chest.

As I turn the handle to my office door, the door is already unlocked. I slowly open the door to reveal a white landscape composed of about one hundred rolls of Charmin. How could I give those bastards the opportunity to toilet paper my office? Ribbons of 2-ply crisscross the room like a highway map, piles of it burying every surface.

Even my nemesis, the yellow couch, has been wound like a mummy with toilet paper. I may leave it like that for a while. *F-you couch.* I stand in the middle of my office and laugh a huge belly-busting laugh. I dig through the coils of TP covering my closet to throw my duffle bag inside.

I then snap a picture of my battleplan whiteboard, complete with a fluted frame of Charmin, with my phone. I grab a nearly complete roll from under my desk and begin unrolling it in the direction of the meeting room. When I am pleased with my toilet paper road, I begin setting up my presentation at the front of the room.

Brad is the first to enter the meeting room with a black-haired woman at his elbow. "Grant, glad to see you are all set up despite the flamboyant reception you received this morning."

"Yes, the guys really got me," I say, laughing slightly. I am already planning payback once I verify if my interior decorators are Nate, James, or both.

"I invited some of the night staff to your presentation since you made the invite list surprisingly small. This is Molina, my wife. She oversees a lot of the night version of Bergan."

"Pleasure to meet you," I say when she offers her

icy hand. I try to shake it, but she has put it out palm down as if expecting me to kiss her rings. The result is a sloppy meeting of the hands. I keep my stiff smile in place.

"You will meet Ryan the Head of QA or Quality Assurance, Lucien the Head of Microbiology, and David the Head of Quality Control. They are battle-ready vampires who specialize in defending against air attacks. You will want cover from the skies but I'm sure you already know that," she says, glaring at me. Her eyes are so odd I can't help but stare. The colors of the pupil and the iris are reversed. It looks like a black hole has crushed her green iris like a paper wad and left it in the middle of her eye.

"They are napping in their offices so they can be here," Brad says adding a glare in my direction, probably for staring at his wife. Brad moves to the windows and pulls the heavy drapes across them. The cinderblock walls, lower lighting, and growing shadows transform the room from sterile meeting room to dungeon. Molina sighs and smiles at her husband. He smiles in return and gives her shoulders a squeeze.

"That's great. I've wanted to meet them in person since we have enjoyed a great working relationship over e-mail. It will also be a relief to have cover from above. If you will excuse me, I'm going to add them to my diagram," I say scrambling to the smart board. I quickly add the night staff to my defense diagram of Bergan.

I put them on the roof and at the top floor windows. People previously stationed there move to the first floor. I had placed who I thought were the best fighters outside the doors on the ground. With a few keystrokes, the warriors are moved outward into the landscaping. Feeling even more confident, I turn back to the room to watch it fill with coworkers.

The last three to arrive are unfamiliar to me so I assume they are from the night staff. They glide into the room with a grace that makes Nate look like a clumsy oaf. The three tall males are dressed in black suits making them look more like secret agents than scientists. The first two have the features of mobsters from the Godfather movies. The third has brown hair and is oddly familiar.

Well, well, well. He's my obtrusive neighbor. I feel a growl rumble in my chest. I cover it with a cough quickly before it is heard over the din in the room. Taking my task list from my pocket, I add a note to ask that he remove watching my wife from his pre-work routine. The trio sits down in chairs along the back wall and stares impassively with eyes like Molina. I snicker to myself as they put on sunglasses in a uniform motion.

"Ladies and Gentlemen, I'd like to get started. Tonight is showtime. We must be in position when the sun sets and since there are no records of last month's battle formations, I've devised a defensive plan of those positions. We must keep the Sluagh from taking control of Bergan or at least getting access to our technical documents," I say.

"There are no battle plans from last month because the Sluagh have not attacked in three months," James interjects sourly.

"There are no records period. That changes tomorrow. We will reconvene here in twenty-four hours for a lessons-learned discussion to be written into standard procedures. Do not worry. This is the last battle where we will be fragmented," I continue.

"I haven't been worried about written records. Are you worried?" Nate quips. His row of colleagues all shake their heads. This is not going well, and my temper is starting to simmer. First, this is a world-ending crisis and now they are acting like insolent teenagers.

I take a deep breath to swallow the growl threatening to leave my chest. "Let's talk about strategy. The Sluagh, as you know, can only see from one side. This means their attack is limited to arrive from the west or the north. Since their fortress is located west of our facility, it is my opinion they will come from that side and circle east. The best lookout perch will be the pond sheltered by large bushes on the northwest corner of the building," I say in Brad's direction.

He nods his head in agreement but, graciously, allows me to continue. "Brad and Nate will take one side of the pond. James and Miles, of the day staff QA, you will take the other side of the pond. Your job will be to judge whether the Sluagh approach from the north or west. You will use the all alert text system on our phones to communicate this.

"Once your area is clear, do not move from it unless you can physically see a colleague struggling in a battle. All information sharing will be via text alert. We cannot leave areas open for the Sluagh to double back on us. That goes for anyone," I say. My temper cools as I start to see nods of agreement boosting my confidence.

"Daytime QC, since there are only two of you, you

will flank the front doors in our front landscaping. This way the team in the bushes can back you up and vice versa. I highly doubt the Sluagh will attack the north side, but I want you there to report if the battle circles around there. On the opposite side, George, I want you to lead your scientific affairs team in the southern bushes unless any of them have animal forms that are too tall. Then they will be with me under the trees on the west side.

"Since the west side is our probable battlefield, I will be there to lead the charge. Regulatory affairs, since you are used to being managed by me, I would like you under the trees as well. Questions from the day staff before I address the stations of the night staff," I say.

Like a DJ at a rave, my statement raises the hands of the entire audience. Ugh. These are educated people who, unlike me, have battled before, why is this so hard? I call on James first.

"I don't shift so I won't be concealed in my assigned space," he says with defiance in his eyes. I don't have time to play his games or interrogate him on his power animal. It teases my curiosity that someone so committed to transforming humans into shifters refuses to use his own shifter form.

"Fine, you are with me in the west trees," I say before he can shoot down any other pieces of the plan or my confidence. Removing my task list once more from my pocket, I make a note to corner James and ask his power animal. If I am going to lead this group, I need him to make a gesture of fealty.

I call on Emily, a shy small associate next. "What about the ladies of HR and document control?" She asks in her quiet delicate voice.

"You will be the only ones locked inside the building," I say as her eyes widen with anger. "You have the most important job of all. If we are defeated and it looks like they are going to breach the building, you are to destroy all our technical data, our lab records, and our network server. We cannot allow them to have access to a means to fund their stay here.

"Without money, they cannot buy weapons or provisions." She's still frowning but says nothing. Hands start descending as people learn what my goal is. I wish to protect our assets while I learn about the enemy. This battle is not about their defeat.

I see one hand is still raised, so I call on Molina.

"What about Paulino's pizza? It is located west of here and I'm worried about Rafaella," she asks.

"I decided to honor the promise to Rosie. She will have all of her boys to defend the pizzeria. I didn't invite them to today's meeting because they will not be at Bergan to help us. They will devise their own strategy based on what they have done in the past," I answer gently. I add a smile to look supportive, but it has a little too much teeth. We are protecting millions of dollars of scientific discovery and they are worried about pizza. Seriously?

"Yeah, where's Josh and Josh from the auto shop? Where's Tyler from Ray's Market? Where's Dr. Van Dijk?" Questions erupt from the crowd as they realize this is a Bergan-only plan.

"I haven't invited any of them. They have their own businesses to protect how they see fit," I say coolly.

"Frankie would be sick over this," I hear

murmuring in the crowd by some unknown person and I see red. I let out a growl and let my muzzle extend.

"If there aren't any more questions and no one wishes to challenge my leadership, I will move onto the placements of the night staff," I say, glaring over the room. I'm met with wide eyes and shocked faces. No one moves. All I can hear is the ticking of my watch and whirring of the ventilation system. I use the silent time to dampen my temper and shift my face back to human form.

"Lucien and David, together you have a staff of 10 members. Could you defend from the roof or do you need more people?" I ask.

"We could defend the skies over the building from there as well. Quite easily indeed," replies Lucien smoothly.

"Great. Then, Ryan, I will need you to take the night staff's Molecular Toxicology and Quality Assurance departments into the trees above me on the west side of the building. I would appreciate the air coverage," I say.

"Grant, could I ask that I join Ryan's group in the trees above? I'd be more effective there than on the ground," Patty asks with her hand raised.

"Sounds reasonable. Ryan, thoughts?"

"I can provide you with coverage but who will cover your family then?" He says smoothly. He crosses one leg over the other while folding his arms across his chest. The pose isn't outwardly aggressive until one combines it with the set of his jaw.

Who does this guy think he is? I see red and fight to resist the change to bear form. I place my claws into my pockets. "They have their instructions as you do. If there are no further questions, I ask you clear your desks of documents. Please check that your desk drawers, closets, and windows are locked with all computers shut down.

"Take a nap or at least rest in the bunks or in your offices. We will reconvene here at 6 o'clock tonight for a light dinner and last-minute preparations," I growl. I snap off the electronics and stomp to my office, leaving everyone staring at my exit.

I slam the door to my office and dig my phone out of my desk. I send a text to Alison to remind her to stay indoors after dark. Our state-of-the-art security system will keep my family safe no matter what that jerk vampire says. Brad and James assured me Sluagh do not break in windows or doors, so historically the humans of this area have been kept inside as their only means of protection.

This is Alison's chance to demonstrate her obedience in the interest of our future. Bergan needs to survive not only for our family's financial future but for the future of those depending on the medicines we create. Alison sees the bigger picture, right?

I get a bunch of emoji icons in response. *What the hell do those mean*? I drop my phone into my pocket, so I don't send an angry text back. It is not her that has me fuming. Hopefully, her hieroglyphs mean she plans to listen better than my employees.

Chapter 23

"That sunset is so gorgeous," I say to Henrik, clasping my hands together. A wild burst of reds, pinks, and oranges explodes through the windows of our home. A kaleidoscope of colors is scattered throughout our first floor where Henrik and I are eating dinner. I walk over to our windows facing our front yard to admire the sky.

"Yeah, it's cool," says Henrik at a neighboring window.

"I wonder what it's doing to the plants out back. I bet the white flowers are tie-dyed with sunbeams," I say crossing back to the kitchen in order to see out of the rear-facing windows.

Each bed of my gardens below has an area asking for attention. My plants have gotten accustomed to my nightly visits under the moonlight. Not only is there no moonlight tonight but there will be no visit. After learning about the Sluagh from Grant, I'm going to stay in and watch a movie with Henrik.

Hopefully, he doesn't pick something scary. I glance down as I trip over a blanket lying haphazardly across the family room floor. The evidence left behind is from my last encounter with Grant. I feel a flush creep up my neck at the memory as I fold it over the couch where it belongs. At least we were decent until we made it into the house.

I can't believe I tried to bribe a bear with a pumpkin. "Oh no, that pumpkin is still there. It's going to rot if I don't retrieve it. I thought a creature would have taken it last night, but I guess it was too big. Henrik, are you sick of making tortellini or will you give me a lesson? I can just taste pumpkin-filled pasta with butter, sage, and warm spices."

"Oh Mom," Henrik groans joining me in the kitchen. "Rosie already works me to the bone. Without the guys, we will have to make the dough ourselves."

"Yes, but we only need enough dough for one pumpkin of filling. We won't be making enough for a whole restaurant, just the three of us. How about ravioli then? I promise to save your fingers for the piano."

"Okay, but we will have extra for ourselves when Dad doesn't show."

"That's not happening anymore. We've worked things out, you have got to trust us," I say giving Henrik my serious-mom-face. He frowns at me and reminds me so much of Grant I want to laugh.

"He's not here now."

"The difference is he told me he wouldn't be here, instead of not showing up while we wait or calling at the last minute with what he would rather be doing. It may not look like it on the outside but it's better on the inside. Speaking of inside, I'm going to go grab that pumpkin before it gets dark. Dad specifically said not to go out after dark tonight for any reason."

"Why?"

"Ahhhhhh, because last night we saw a bear. We need to figure out how to coexist with the bear before getting too close." With that, I slip out the back door and onto the balcony, so I don't have to elaborate on my story. Henrik is super sharp, and I have decided it is not going to be me who tells him his father is part bear, or sometimes a bear, or whatever.

I take a deep breath of autumn air and stretch up toward the vibrant sky. I stare past my fingers at the bands of color and wait for the peace to wash over me only nature can bring. When it doesn't come, I bring my hands back down and frown. I need to get my toes in the dirt, just for a few seconds. Score! My gardening apron hanging crookedly on a post from the previous night.

As I tie it to my waist, I pet the little plant that has been living in one of the pockets. I would have to give it a home tonight as well. It is cruel to keep it living in a pocket. With a wave to Henrik watching at the windows, I leap over the side of the balcony.

Once my toes hit the ground, I sense something is wrong. The ground sends tiny vibrations of warning to me via my feet. It is decidedly colder down here. There is a small current of air coming from the direction of the house behind me. My subconscious pricks at me; the direction is unnatural. The structure itself would block any gentle breeze. The hairs on my arm begin to stand on end so I cautiously walk away from the house to pick up the pumpkin.

I must fight the urge to turn toward the house to run up the stairs because part of me is too scared to face whatever is waiting against the house. I clutch the pumpkin to my chest like a security blanket and take a deep breath. *This is my territory.* Still, facing the end of my yard, I call out; "Who's out there?"

Two wolves, a shiny black one and a smaller gray one, emerge from behind a tree to stalk me. They are snarling and baring their teeth. I am frozen solid for a second. I start to slowly back away from the wolves as they split their paths. Each is approaching at a forty-five-degree angle from me. I need to get out of their trap before they pounce. I do a mental inventory of my pockets, realizing I have no sharp objects I can use to fight them off.

My only option is to run but I'm moving slowly to not provoke the wolves into pouncing. I'm certain the black one is faster than me. In studying her, I have taken my eyes off the gray one for too long and he has caught up to me. I sense his position when I feel his velvety fur against my legs.

Survival instincts finally kick in and I leap backwards to catch a support beam of the deck with one hand. I curl myself into a ball in the hopes I am high enough to reach the base of the deck with my legs. No luck. The wolves circle the base of my pole and I begin to scream.

"Mom, where are you?" I hear Henrik call out.

"I'm below the deck. I am surrounded by wolves. Don't come down here," I yell in response.

I see Henrik lean over the railing. His face is pulled with fear. He reaches down toward me, but I am too low to reach. I clumsily climb up the pole toward his outstretched hand, still holding the pumpkin in one arm.

"Don't worry. Wolves can't climb up poles. Is the gate closed and locked at the steps? I will keep an eye on them, but I want a way to slow them down if they use the stairs to get to us," I say to him. At this point, I'm not sure who I am reassuring, Henrik or myself. I smile at the wolves nervously. The gray one is still growling. The black one isn't even looking at me.

I don't have time to ponder wolf psychology before something grabs the waistband of my leggings and yanks me off my perch. I hit the ground so hard the wind knocks out of me. I get raked across the gravel as I'm pulled vertical. I lunge forward at the waist and I release my pumpkin to slap the ground before my head connects with it.

I use all my abdominal strength to lift my top half and instantly wish I hadn't. I am face-to-face with the stuff of nightmares. Fathomless black eyes bore into me as a lipless smile sends chills down my spine. Inside the smile, a long black tongue runs across tiny pearl points with greed. I hear myself scream and see my fists flailing helplessly in my line-of-sight.

The gray wolf lunges at the phantom and gets smacked into the house. He lands with a grunt; his limbs contorted at unnatural angles. The black wolf circles around to stand over the smaller wolf. Her ears flatten against her head as she growls. The phantom begins to chuckle. "Do you really want to charge at me, bitch? I can break you one-handed as well," it sneers at the wolf. I get a blast of rotten breath as he speaks. It smells of decay, increasing my fear. If only I wasn't held aloft, I could ground myself and drain my fear into the earth.

A spade flies at the creature from my peripheral vision and knocks lightly into its shoulder. "Let go of my mother," commands Henrik from the bottom of the stairs. Time seems to slow as he approaches the phantom and my fear reaches panic levels. The phantom gets a gleeful look in his eyes and floats us toward Henrik. *No, no, no, no, no!* I begin to tear at the phantom in earnest.

"No, Henrik. Go inside. Go call your Dad. Henrik, you need to run. RUN!" I scream hysterically. It takes all my strength not to pass out as I see the intent in the phantom's eyes. He wants us both.

"Well, look here. It must be a BOGO sale on witches. I have been watching little miss golden stars, but I never knew about you, Boy. Yes, come closer. I want to see the golden stars in your eyes. Stars that are to be my ticket back home. An extra ticket means I can bring you back to the General. He will be pleased if I get him back to the Fae as well. He will raise my station for this gift. Yes, child, try to attack. You don't want Mommy damaged, do you?" the phantom taunts.

His voice holds discordant hisses and wheezes in pitches I know hurt Henrik's ears. I watch my son wince with each word until the final question. With the last question, the phantom's long tongue reaches out and licks at my ear. I fight and twist as acidic saliva burns my neck. I can barely feel the burning. The pain comes from the deafening sizzling of my skin as it is so close to my ear.

"Henrik, no!" I scream but it's too late. He is seeing red. He can no longer reach the rational parts of his brain. I recognize his mask of fury because it is identical to the one his father wears often. Henrik is falling into the monster's trap and I feel helpless. It is as if the phantom's claws are already deep into Henrik.

"Beautiful, my little witch, your skin tastes as sweet as your sadness," the phantom says, pushing his face next to mine. This is too much for Henrik and he lunges at the phantom. At that moment, the black wolf jumps on the backside of the phantom to aid my son. The phantom clutches Henrik by the shoulder with a claw, cackling wildly.

Black claws pierce Henrik. Blood begins to trickle down his arm. Henrik fights the hold madly while crying out in pain. A cold wind swirls around us as the phantom flaps his wings. The movement dislodges the black wolf and we start to fly away. We are so heavy our group is only two feet off the ground, maybe even less.

"Fight Henrik! Grab at the ground to make yourself heavy," I yell. I tear at the grass as it whizzes past. The plants rise to my rescue by reaching toward me. The softer plants are able to wrap themselves around my wrists and ankles. Their pain as they are torn from the ground radiates around us, shaking me to my core.

Tears fly from my eyes to splatter around them as I mourn their sacrifice. New plants emerge everywhere I touch and instantly flower leaving a technicolor trail behind us. Henrik follows my lead clutching at the ground, but it slips through his fingers. The phantom starts to puff clouds of putrid breath as he struggles against the plants.

We slow down enough I can watch the wolves. The black one is trying to lift the gray one with her muzzle, but it is almost her size. The gray one lifts his head and snaps at her until she stops to turn at us. She then takes off at full speed around to the front of the house. The gray one sadly watches us float away and howls.

Chapter 24

Prebattle meeting. Check. Sweat suits donned for easy changing. Check. Stations manned or womaned. Check. Sunset. Check. I take a huge breath of air. I have never done this. I didn't even fight other kids in elementary school. My family's faces at the breakfast table flash before my eyes. I've got to save Bergan to provide for them.

I scan for Sluagh, from the skies to the ground and the north to the south. Repeat. My hands are clammy with nervousness. Sweat trickles between my shoulder blades to flow down my back. Breathe. I see a moving shape appear along the horizon. I recognize it as my friend who regularly spies on my wife. The she-wolf is running at top speed with her tongue hanging out of the side of her mouth. I walk to the edge of the trees to get a closer look.

"Rosie," James whispers. I raise my fist to keep the others in position as James and I approach her. We crouch in front of her. She's babbling but we can barely hear her voiceless wheezes.

"They have them. We must go. They have them," the wolf says breathlessly. I watch her sides heave and bellow with each word. There are long bloody slashes along her sides as if she has been caught in the jaws of a shark.

"Rosie?" The two women are thick as thieves so it

is confusing as to why Rosie would spy outside instead of visiting my house in human form. Rosie and I have a cordial friendship too. Why would she keep her identity from me? Brad identified her as a shifter, but I should have asked her role in the pack at the pizza party. Oh my God, she was mated to the former leader. I'm frozen by the realization she knew Alison was a leader's mate at my turning. In frustration, Rosie shifts just her face to human, keeping her wolf body and head.

"The Sluagh have grabbed Alison and Henrik. Matteo is hurt. This is wrong. It's all wrong. You got it wrong," she says with a sob.

The gravity of her message hits me like a ton of bricks. My little family is in the claws of a nightmare. They are so fragile. There is no way they will free themselves. I am their only hope at survival. I need to get there. I kick myself for not being there in the first place. This is what Rosie meant by protecting my family when we were at the pizza lunch at Bergan.

She knew my family would be targeted because her family had been under constant fire from both Vincenzo and Frankie being the pack leaders. She was probably patrolling my yard with Matteo, making sure Alison and Henrik are safe inside. I should have seen they were safe with my own eyes too. Maybe I would have been there to face the Sluagh instead of two kids with their moms.

I feel a rush of warm air as we are joined by David, Lucien, and Ryan. My jaw drops. This is why they wanted to patrol the rooftops. They can fly. Giant black bat wings have emerged from slits in their dinner jackets. I had wondered why they were heading into battle in tuxes but now I see the versatility. A boulder sinks in my gut. I have missed a lot in my preparations. To cover my missteps and to take charge, I start firing orders.

"Lucien go to Dr. Van Dijk's and take him to my house. Together, you need to triage Matteo. Do whatever it takes to help the kid," I say to him.

He doesn't answer me but looks to Ryan. Ryan nods slightly and Lucien takes flight. I'm instantly incensed by the insolence but there are bigger issues to tackle.

"David, can you take Rosie back to Paulino's? I bet Rafaella can patch her up and then I'll text Lucien to bring Matteo there once the doctor gets him stable," James says.

"Do it," I growl at James and David. James takes out his phone while David takes to the skies. James points toward his motorcycle and I nod in agreement that he should get it. This group is moving now.

"Looks like you are going to get a closer look at my wife after all," I sneer at Ryan.

"Fuck off," he replies.

"Grab your nightcrawlers. We need to go save her," I say taking out my phone. I send out a text telling everyone we are going to the Sluagh fortress.

"By the time you bumble over there, she will be gone," Ryan says and disappears right before my eyes. He reappears behind me and wraps his arms around mine. "Arms straight out and think light thoughts, Pooh Bear," he adds before launching us into the air. We fly as fast as a jet toward my house.

"You drop me, and you will pay, you overgrown mosquito," I taunt as my house comes into view.

Ryan chuckles and unceremoniously drops me onto

my top balcony. He gracefully lands beside a smashed pumpkin at the bottom of the stairs. I lumber my way down using my clawed feet and hands. At the bottom, I find Ryan on his hands and knees looking at a burn hole in the yard.

"What are you looking for?"

"Bloodstones. These are burn marks from Sluagh saliva. Rocks coated with witch blood and Sluagh saliva capture their magic. They can act as a homing beacon for us. I was also looking for human pieces to see if we were too late. There aren't any so I think there is still time. What is your wife's elemental magic basis?"

"Uh, she smells like bergamot?"

"Really? You live with her for how many years and that's all you got?"

"What? She doesn't have elemental magic."

"Actually, she's a moonchild with magic communicating to the Earth and creating plant life," Matteo calls from his pile against the house, Gran, Lucien, David, and Dr. Van Dijk standing in a huddle beside him.

"How can you say that? She's perfectly normal," I reply. She has kept her secret since childhood. I will not give it away in my first week trusted to keep it. It pricks my pride that Matteo seems to have much more information on Alison. Could she have shared her plant magic with them before me?

"Henrik is a moon child too, but his magic has an air basis. His music is not only beautiful, but it can be hypnotic too. Right Gran?" Matteo replies.

What?! They are talking about something much bigger than Alison's super gardening. If Alison knew

Henrik has some extra ability, she would have told me when she revealed her own secret. How could I miss how special my family is?

"You are going to be okay, kid. Thanks for trying to rescue her," Ryan says to Matteo. Ryan walks over to Matteo and pats him on the back.

"Yes. He's right Grant," Gran says, approaching me. I look at her face to see if she's kidding or serious. It strikes me then. Her eyes are familiar because of the stars in the center. She has silver stars in the center of her violet eyes. They match the size and shape of the golden stars in Alison's eyes...in Henrik's eyes. "Now we are getting somewhere," she adds as I continue to stare.

"Look, there's a trail of flowers leading through the woods in the direction of the castle," Ryan says from behind a hoop house.

"I've got to save her," I say, starting to run to the end of the yard.

Ryan rolls his eyes as I pass. "How about you hitchhike again?"

I stop because I'm already winded. *Why couldn't I have manifested as a cheetah*? I put my arms out and Ryan hooks me up again. "Can't you do the flashing thing, so we appear there?" I grouch.

"Nope," Ryan says after liftoff. "I can only flash to places within my sightline. I can go alone or with my true mate and sorry, Papa Bear is not my type. It also takes a tremendous amount of energy, not that carrying your bulk is easy."

"Then why the pet names?" I sneer.

"I'm trying them on you like a fashion show. I want to see what sticks...like honey, Pooh. Pooh is the exact nickname for you. You are definitely Pooh," he says, thoughtfully.

"Oh really?"

"Yeah," he says, "because you have it all and decided to poo, poo, poo all over it."

"Not funny."

"I'm not trying to be. You will be punished enough if you lose her tonight. Trust me, I know."

"I will get there in time—"

"Thanks to me. Thanks to Rosie. Remember who watched over your mate while you were playing soldier. As a shifter, you will have a long lifespan to regret the loss. Ask James."

I stash the vampire's lecture in the proverbial circular file with a note to learn more about James. I continue to fume as we follow the carpet of wildflowers. "I can't believe she made this. All this life created out of nothing but her touch," I murmur in disbelief. Why did I take her for granted? How can I return to our empty house surrounded by the evidence I lost the most important people in my life?

"Probably grabbing at the dirt with all her magic trying to save her child or her own life caused the earth to reach back to save her. Why would you ever jeopardize someone so precious as bait?"

"I didn't use her as bait," I reply in horror. In truth, I didn't see who she is and everyone else did. I have a magical rose with the ability to touch the heart of everyone she comes across and I take her for granted. I am haunted by the image of her hunched over the sink on our bathroom counter.

The pain I saw in her eyes was powerful enough to call a Sluagh. Pain I had put there and everyone saw that too. I feel a tidal wave of shame.

"That's not what I saw," Ryan says while dropping me in front of a condemned stone building.

"I forget you love to play Peeping Tom."

"What? Are you calling the guy who flew you over here, so you have a chance of saving your wife a Peeping Tom?"

"Are there many men using binoculars to watch my wife in the evenings?"

"Oh, you mean, watching the Sluagh hiding around your house since you moved in. Pretty slick installing motion-activated lights to keep them close enough to watch but too far away to snatch anyone unless it's the new moon."

"You lie. There is not a Sluagh hanging around my house."

"That witch's loneliness has filled the skies since you got here. Every Vampire, Sluagh, and Gremlin for a hundred miles could hear her heart calling for you."

"What did you call her?" I hiss as I start to see red.

"Are you kidding me? That's why your yard is Grand Central Station after dark. Rosie and her kids have been taking lead on patrolling your yard. When you started lurking in your own trees, I assumed it was at your request. I couldn't understand how you could put her through all that pain to get rid of the Fae. If you are our destined leader, why didn't you sacrifice yourself first?

"I got my answer when I listened to your battleplan. Your greed is more powerful than your feelings for her. Protect Bergan's money from the Fae, laughable. Why have stupid human money when they can have a witch's soul to get back home?" Ryan lectures.

"I didn't think they would value Alison. There were no instructions, standard operating procedures or battleplans. I couldn't get straight answers from the ones in power. I had to learn from the internet about the Sluagh. Attacking from the west, blind in one eye, connected to the evil eye, and other facts were from Google!" I fire back.

"Who did you ask? You didn't ask anyone for help except Brad. You are so elitist that only the CEO's advice is good enough for you. James told me how rude you were to Gran. She's a witch and could have helped Alison. You shut her out," Ryan yells.

I slug him. Right across his smug face. I hear a crack as my fist connects and his head whips to one side. I instantly pounce him, and we go tumbling to the ground. I'm trying to shift but I'm too angry.

I will not be judged by some horror movie knock-off. As we wrestle on the ground, I hear the approach of the herd of wild animals, led by a motorcycle. I turn to see the entire town approaching us. I look back at Ryan to see his eyes are now glowing red and his mouth is full of long, white fangs.

Chapter 25

The building we are being dragged toward looks bombed out like those found in Chernobyl, not Strawberry, Kentucky. The large stone ruin appears from behind a grassy hill. It is the shape of a dumbbell with two taller portions on the ends and a one-story section in the middle. As we are towed to it, more details are revealed. The top is jagged where stones have released their mortar and leaped over the side.

The suicidal stones lay in heaps around the building as a warning to other stones hoping to escape. The windows on the bottom level are covered with clean plywood planks, giving the building a polka dot belt. The top windows are without glass creating the illusion of a screaming multi-eyed businessman with his shoulders hunched over because his belt is too tight.

The demon begins to cackle with glee, shaking us slightly as we hang suspended from its claws. A new burst of energy from seeing his destination helps to overcome his exhaustion.

I feel us accelerate and look over to my son. Henrik is still grabbing at the ground but crying hysterically. The fragile brave shell from our yard has been shattered leaving behind my little boy. I reach over and take his hand. He stops clawing to look over at me. "Mommy," he croaks. He has been screaming for so long his voice is gone, and his shoulder wound is no longer bleeding. I can feel his energy draining and despair set in.

"I'll figure this out. As long as we are together, I will protect you. We aren't done yet. Please mentally stay with me," I plead with him. He sniffs and nods at me in response. My mind begins to race with people who could help us. Grant is undoubtedly fighting more of these fiends.

When he comes home in the morning, he will instantly know what happened. Henrik left the back door open. If Grant checks the alarm system on his phone, he will see the door is open. If he's fighting for his life, he's probably not checking his phone. I need to keep us alive until morning when he can rescue us.

I think of our friends at the pizzeria. They are closer than where Grant is located at Bergan Pharma. Gran could magic away from this phantom, I just know it. How would I get them a message of our location? If only I had a messenger, like the wolves in our yard. My hopelessness evaporates. The postures of the wolves during our encounter start to make sense. The wolves were defending us. There is no way they were wild wolves. They were either pets of my creepy neighbor or maybe shifters.

I replay the events in the yard in my head. They were always snarling toward something behind me. Was it my stupid luck or even negligence that I interrupted their battle with a demon? In any event, I have a friend in the black wolf. I can only hope she is a shifter who can communicate my abduction to the good guys. Henrik senses my increased spirits and I shoot him a secret smile. If I can keep us alive, help is on the way.

The phantom jolts us as he heads toward a second-story window on the right side of the building. We bluntly hit the window frame as he sails through one of the open holes. The impact swings Henrik's legs in an unnatural way and I hear a grating as his left femur shatters.

My limbs fare better but because I'm folded in half, my head slams against the stone. I fight to clear the stars from my vision. A wave of nausea makes the room spin. I close my eyes. I use my yoga breathing to center myself.

When I open my eyes, Henrik is sitting on the stone floor. He is shackled at the wrists by shiny chains bolted to the wall. His left leg hangs lifelessly on the floor but there is no blood seeping through his jeans. He has calmed considerably and is staring at me with wild eyes. The phantom must be still holding me, so I begin to twist and fight.

"There, there, my little witch," the phantom coos at me. "The Sluagh General will take care of you soon enough. He will love his present and all this will be over. As in your life will soon be over." He adds a cackle at the end and yanks my hair to pull me to a standing position. I recoil in disgust as he crowds my space to hang me from suspended chains. His putrid breath fans over my head as I am pressed against him.

My nausea from the head injury comes back with a vengeance. I wish my stomach was full so I can throw up all over him. I dry-heave and retch as he presses his bony frame against mine. I'm finally tethered, and he steps back to admire his handiwork giving me relief.

"Maybe I should keep you for myself, little Witch. You would make such a fun playmate before you send me home," the Sluagh says, tapping his chin with a long black claw. He gazes at my suspended body with glee, his eyes burning me from head to toe. I let him taunt me to keep his attention off Henrik. If he wants to play this intimidation game all night, he will be rudely interrupted when help arrives. The Sluagh floats back over to me and sticks out his long black tongue.

I instinctively shrink away from the wiggling phallus. The tongue starts at my ear and travels down to the neckline of my shirt, leaving a trail of acid burns on my skin. Any normal person would feel the agony of the burns, and I am grateful for my condition. I barely feel his ministrations. I send him a glare to allow him to see he doesn't hurt me. I want to tear him limb from limb and I feel my temper rise.

I take a deep breath and find my center. I start to mentally catalog everything in the room, from my pockets' contents to the clumps of silt on the floor. The room is lit with torches casting eerie shadows over the bare stone walls. Torches line the hall outside our door. I guess they are saving money by not having electricity. The dim light is a blessing to me. I'm able to see better and there are no electric lights buzzing to bother me.

Rings and posts dot the walls on all sides as well as the ceiling so someone could be chained in a myriad of poses. There is a bar-covered window between our cell and the cell next door. Chained spread-eagle to the wall is a blonde woman. Her head hangs motionlessly so her long hair hangs to her knees. She shows no signs of life through all the commotion in our cell. As I continue to stare at her, she lifts her head slightly to reveal her face. A beautiful set of brown human eyes stare back at me.

"No, I can't jeopardize a rise in station for an ordinary witch. A higher station means higher quality

Fae to play games. I'm going to get the General, now. Just hang out for a bit," the phantom cackles to himself. The wheezing laughter follows him out of the door. It closes with a resounding thud. Henrik begins to cry softly.

"I'm sorry little flower but I have need of you," I whisper downward. I fold my legs upward as the little plant in my pocket bends toward my feet. I use my toes to pluck a few leaves off the plant with each foot. I continue to fold myself in half to wedge the leaves between the cuffs and my hands. I shimmy my shoulders to twist my wrists in the cuffs.

The waxy leaves are minced into a slippery paste, lubricating my wrists. I use my double-jointed knuckles to force my hands out of the cuffs. I drop into a pile on the floor and make a vow to yoga more than once per day if I get out of this alive. When I lift my head, Henrik is staring at me in shock. I beam at him and I am rewarded with renewed hope in his smile.

"I'm not sure what this does but I got it from Gran," I whisper to him. I pull the bag of magic from my apron and extract the vials. I vow to get lessons from Gran if this works and I see tomorrow.

"No, no, no, Mom. You have got to go. Go and get Dad. Leave me to get Dad," Henrik pleads. I ignore his urgent whispers. I splash droplets of the water on our faces and necks. It acts as an adhesive when I spread the salty ash on it. Besides a little sparkle, it is invisible.

"Gran says this is powerful or gives us power. Do you feel anything different?" I am answered with a searing glare. I shrug my shoulders and work a few leaves from my apron into Henrik's cuffs.

"I'm not double-jointed like you. I'm not bendy at

all. In fact, I can't feel my leg! I can't get out of these things. I need Dad to get the key," Henrik says beginning to cry again.

Crash! The door explodes open and I'm hopeful help has arrived. My happy bubble is popped when the dust settles. The Sluagh is back with an even bigger Sluagh behind him. This bigger Sluagh must be the General who our phantom was referring to earlier. Their lipless smiles are dripping black drool. They rub their claws together in unison. I shift my position to block Henrik.

"Mommy, Mommy, I can't Mommy. Go and get Daddy. I need my Daddy," the smaller Sluagh taunts in a high-pitched voice. They both throw their heads back to laugh. I start to measure how many steps it would take to reach the window. We aren't higher up than my balcony so I know I can make the jump. I have second thoughts when I realize I would be leaving Henrik behind. Henrik is right about his hands. His frequent piano playing has built up the muscles around his finger joints so they will not fold themselves small enough to get out of the cuffs.

"Well, Boy, you have your wish. I smell the shifters. I bet we have a menagerie on the front lawn," the General sneers.

"How will we defend against them? There's only the two of us?" The smaller Sluagh replies with panic.

"Who cares? We will be home before they can throw the first punch," the General answers. He grabs my shoulders with a viselike grip and throws me aside as if I'm no more than a ragdoll. He crawls closer to Henrik to get right in his face. "You want to say goodbye, don't you, Boy? Your fear smells delicious. I bet you will reach an intoxicating level when you see how weak Daddy really is," he purrs in Henrik's face.

He stands and releases Henrik's chains from the wall. He tries to lead Henrik out by the leash, but Henrik's broken leg keeps him from being able to walk. The General grabs his shirt collar and lifts Henrik off his feet.

"We are heading out for a going-away party. I suggest you have your party here and get out before the shifters enter. See you in the Fae," the General calls as he floats out of the window.

I'm left with my original kidnapper. Crouched in the corner, I wait for him to approach me. He's still smiling and rubbing his hands together. He floats over and chuckles as I gather my legs beneath me. I wait for him to bend down to grab me. Crack! I kick my leg over my head with all the strength I possess. My bare heel connects with his jaw and bucks his head backward.

I scramble to get past him and to run toward the door when he releases an ear-piercing screech. I am paralyzed by pain in my ears as the sound rattles around my skull. The pressure builds as I feel fluid collecting in my ear canals to protect my eardrums. I cannot resist the urge to cover my ears with my hands and bend down to cover my head. Nothing helps to dampen the terrible sound.

The sound stops but there is now a persistent ringing in my ears. My feet leave the floor as I am jerked backward by my elbows. I twist and fight to get free. My balance is now off due to the damage inside my ears and my movements are uncoordinated. In addition, I feel a strange pain in the tips of my fingers and toes.

The phantom easily hauls me around to face him. He transfers both of my elbows into one of his long claws. The claws bite into my skin but it barely registers compared to the pain in my ears, my feet, and my fingertips. I'm baffled by his ability to inflict pain on areas he's not touching when I have such a high pain tolerance.

He breathes a cloud of stale breath over me as he blatantly ogles me. I try to shrink into myself, but I'm held in a way that thrusts my chest out toward him. His free black claw extends toward me as his eyes lock on mine. The claw hooks under the left strap of my shirt and snaps it away.

He then traces my collar bone across my chest to the second strap. I grind my teeth as it snips the second strap. The front of my shirt flops forward in defeat, baring my breasts to him. I hold his gaze and refuse to let him sense anything other than anger. *I will not give him the satisfaction of fear*.

"Such a pity I will not have more time with you, my little witch. I bet this glistening skin would look so beautiful with red stripes from my whip. I would love to hear you cry out as it cracks against your skin. Would your scars be soft?

"When would that hopeless sadness radiate from you again? It has been so sweet to drink in your calls each night. I have dreamt of getting my hands on you, ready for this moment. Yet, I smell no fear. I bet you will soon fear me, my pet," he whispers in my ear.

His long tongue snakes out of his mouth to lick along my torso. I fight to hold still and think of my next move as his tongue slides upward. He moans as it travels along my ribs to my neck. I can barely feel his violations so if I don't watch it, I can ignore it completely.

He leans in to bring his mouth closer and he wraps his tongue around my neck. The tiny teeth of the Sluagh scratch at my skin. The pain in my feet intensifies and spreads to my legs. The pain is deep in my bones and I can no longer ignore it. I try desperately to center myself, but my pelvis begins to ache. How is the Sluagh doing this? I can't control my fear as my imagination takes over. What is he preparing my pelvis to do?

I watch his eyelashes flutter in ecstasy, and I hope Grant is saving Henrik from experiencing this abuse outside. I hold onto the hope to dilute my fear. After retracting his tongue to swallow, he sticks it out again to trace under my chin and along my cheek. Fear coats his face as he jolts backward and falls to the floor. I am released as he shakes and seizes uncontrollably. He tries to howl but no sound emerges, contorting his face into horrible expressions of pain. He claws at his mouth in desperation, leaving long gashes along his jaw.

In the distance, I hear Henrik scream. I step away from the Sluagh and toward the window between the two cells. "I will come back for you," I tell the blonde. She is watching me with shocked eyes, and I don't blame her. My voice sounds low and growling to my ears.

"Hurry, the next new moon brings the army. I'm the entertainment," she says softly. Her voice is delicate and beautiful. However, the tone is marred by her sadness.

I nod and try to open my door. My fingers aren't able to bend, and I wonder if there are side effects to

Gran's magic that I should have asked about before wearing it. I look over to the Sluagh. He has stopped seizing and his limbs are desiccating into silt. He is a torso and head surrounded by piles of the ash. I decide it is totally worth my discomfort in my hands until I double over in pain. I hear Henrik scream again and I falter toward the window.

Chapter 26

"Well, well, well, an audience just for me. I have a new ventriloquist act for tonight. Say hello to my little dummy," I hear the Sluagh call over to us. He is hovering between the first- and the second-story of the building. Candlelight from inside shows us that he holds Henrik by the shirt collar as a human shield. The Sluagh's long black claw is tracing little scrapes along Henrik's throat. I growl as Henrik's eyes glow gold with fear.

The Sluagh is at least seven feet tall and Henrik looks so small compared to the creature. The Fae wears a tattered black robe that swirls below them like a storm cloud. It has the illusion of being made of smoke in the moonless dark night.

"Say hello, Dummy," the Sluagh hisses into Henrik's ear. A long black tongue snakes out of his mouth and flicks Henrik's earlobe. Henrik screams in pain as his delicate ear sizzles with acid burns. The monster takes a deep breath to smell the fear radiating from my son and then throws his head back in laughter.

Ryan and I scramble to get to our feet. The Sluagh is too high for me to reach, even if I jump. I rip my sweatshirt over my head and shift my upper body. I grow an extra two feet in height as my frame fills out. My chest is now barrel-shaped and covered with thick brown fur. Claws that rival the Sluagh's extend from paws, which are twice the size of my human hands. My narrow nose elongates into a muzzle full of fangs. Ryan gives me a nod and begins to rise in order to crash into the Sluagh. Once they hit the ground, I plan to tear that thing to shreds.

"Tsk, tsk, tsk, flying rat. This is my toy. I plan on ripping out his heart at the end of the performance so you can't interrupt. Not a flap closer or I will have to end early," the Sluagh says as he digs the tracing claw into Henrik's chest. Ryan lowers himself to the ground with his hands raised in surrender.

A small trickle of blood starts to stain Henrik's shirt as the Sluagh removes his claw. Henrik screams and struggles in a frenzy. The Sluagh licks the blood from his claw with reverence. He moans while his eyelashes flutter.

"Hysterical fear is bringing out your inner witch, Boy. You taste delicious," the Sluagh hisses.

A loud roar comes from the window behind the Sluagh. Everyone looks at me and I frown in confusion.

"Ooooh, Daddy is mad enough to throw his roar around. Who's trying to upstage my ventriloquist act? Good thing Daddy's too small to take on me," the Sluagh says to Henrik.

With a deafening roar, a white cloud bursts from the fortress window slamming into the Sluagh from behind. The three bodies are cast to the ground. The white cloud lands on top with a thud and looks to me with golden eyes. On closer inspection, I find sharp claws, pointed teeth, and furious eyes. It is a polar bear, the size of a mid-sized sedan. Whatever happened inside that fortress, she's pissed. I can only hope she is a shifter and on our side.

With another earth-shaking roar, the polar bear hooks her left paw to the underside of Henrik's waist. She picks up Henrik from the tangle of limbs and tosses him at me. Henrik flies into my arms and bowls us over from the bear's force. Ryan steps in front of us. I'm unsure whether he's guarding us from the Sluagh or from the bear.

The polar bear stomps her large paws onto the Sluagh's spine, so she is facing to the west of where we are standing. With each step, we hear the cracking of the Sluagh being squashed like a bug. She lowers her muzzle to use her teeth to tear off the Sluagh's arm. An arc of acidic blood sprays onto the grass. The grass blades curl around the droplets and sink into the ground.

Beads of black acid sit on top of the bear's dense fur. She shakes her muzzle upward flinging the arm about ten feet away. The Sluagh's wing receives the same treatment as the arm and joins it on the grass. The Sluagh lets out a deafening screech and tries to wiggle free, however, the bear is too heavy to be dislodged.

Henrik covers his ears and buries his head in my chest at the noise. The bear looks directly at him and roars. Then she clamps her teeth on the Sluagh's neck puncturing his windpipe. The phantom's sound is reduced to wheezing. She pulls and tugs with her muzzle while her paws stay anchored on his spine until his head goes flying off toward the fortress.

The Sluagh corpse is twitching as it uses its remaining life force to try to locate its missing pieces. The bear makes easy work of the still attached wing and arm, sending them sailing toward the grass in the opposite direction of their matches.

She scrapes her paws under her vast weight like a cat in a litter box, shredding the remaining body into ribbons. Henrik lifts his head from my chest and the bear winks at him. She roars once more and shakes her fur sending the remaining acid beaded on her fur into the grass.

I shift back to be fully human and put out my arm for everyone to stay back. Could it be? I recognize those golden stars dancing in the eyes of the bear. I lift Henrik off me and place him beside Ryan just in case.

I take a few hesitant steps toward the bear and extend my hand. I hesitantly use it to cup her face. Beneath my hand, her muzzle recedes leaving the sweet face of my wife on the head of a polar bear. She nuzzles her cheek in my hand as her eyes well with tears. She starts to bend down, but I wrap my arms around her front legs until she stands tall. I lower myself to one knee before her.

"This is your true leader. I kneel before your true heroine and my queen," I call out.

Ryan is first to walk up to us clutching Henrik. Together they kneel beside me. "I will continue to watch over you. You have the fealty of the vampires," he says.

James dismounts from his motorcycle and comes over. He has Nate padding in snow leopard form and Brad in his lion form at his side. Together they kneel behind Ryan. "We will proudly serve you. You have all the resources of Bergan at your disposal," Brad announces.

One by one all the shifters and vampires kneel to swear allegiance to my wife. She looks so majestic sitting astride the remains of her enemy with her followers bowing before her. Henrik is looking around with wild eyes and I make a note to explain all of this to him.

I almost lost him when I have wasted so much of his childhood. Ever observant, Alison catches the look I exchange with my son. She digs her claws into clean dirt and places it onto Henrik's injured shoulder. The slashes begin to heal immediately as they drink the soil. He smiles at the wound and lunges at her, wrapping his arms around the bear. I laugh as his hug only reaches to her sides.

With a distant rumble, Gran and Ray bring up the Paulinos' van. Ray hops out and runs around to help Gran out of the van. She uses her cane to hobble over the uneven grass toward us. With Ray's help, she kneels before Alison. Alison bows her head as Gran returns to standing.

"We brought shovels, Bergan sweat suits, and transport. The Sluagh must be dismembered, buried, and then have their graves covered with rocks. You took care of the dismembering part but if I can, I suggest you give out the orders for clean up before attempting to shift back. It can be quite debilitating," Gran says gently to Alison.

"Thank you, Gran. Henrik's leg is probably broken. Could you examine it? I can heal cuts but not broken bones. He may need Dr. Van Dijk," Alison asks in a growling bear voice.

"Flower, his leg is broken," Gran says crouching next to Henrik. "Brad, could you find a stick long enough for me to immobilize it?"

"Ray, will you distribute the sweat suits and then assist James? James, will you retrieve the shovels and lead the clean-up efforts? Do you think the vampires would mind helping with the digging?" Alison says from her bear's muzzle. The last part is directed toward Ryan.

"We would be glad to. I'm Ryan, your neighbor, by the way. Before you swipe those claws at me, I was watching the Sluagh hunting you, not spying on you. I have already been beaten up for it by another bear tonight," Ryan says with his hands up in surrender. Alison nods at him as he backs away.

"Felines, please refrain from shifting and help with the digging until the Sluagh is buried. Then I will need further assistance from you. There's another girl in there. She's trapped. We need to get to her now. I believe all the Sluagh here are dead, but I don't want any surprises," Alison projects over the crowd.

"The first group of non-feline shifters please accompany Grant to the van to shift, recover, and dress. Grant, will you keep Henrik at your side and be the ones to use the van to ferry everyone back to Bergan who originated there?"

"Dr. Van Dijk is at Paulino's helping Matteo with his injuries. Should I take Henrik there?"

"Yes, he needs a doctor. Drop him off with the first group of personnel," Gran says.

She should be traumatized or at least exhausted by her ordeal, but her eyes are clear, and her voice is strong. Everyone springs into action at her requests as if she were barking out orders. Her gentle demeanor doesn't camouflage the strength of her polar bear form.

"M'lady, if you please, we would like to bury the torso. It is still, um, that is, um, you are still..." Lucien stammers as he approaches with a shovel.

Alison looks down and laughs as if she's perched on the carpet he's trying to vacuum. She gently steps a few steps away and rubs her paws on fresh grass. The blades reach up to clean the black blood off her paws and then draw it into the ground, leaving a fresh soil behind. Lucien and I stare in amazement. How did I not notice her magic before moving to Strawberry?

I carry Henrik to where several of the shifters have changed and are clumped together in the back of the van. I lift Henrik into the front passenger seat. I start to catalog the evening for the lessons I need to learn from Alison.

I look in the rearview mirror to see my polar bear wandering from group to group organizing people. She checks in with each person before moving on, assuring she includes everyone.

In trying to do everything, I was excluding people as if they were just details. However, I am not certain how Alison's tenure as the leader will play out either. When the adrenaline wears off and her sensory abnormalities show their colors, will she be able to handle the pack? It's easy to lead others as a bloodthirsty polar bear, but what about as a mild-mannered homeschool mom?

Chapter 27

As I watch my family drive away in a company van, I am relieved they are away from this place. The black magic surrounding the building is beating at my temples. It has crept into my bones and they have started to ache. There's a chill to the magic that has the vampires shivering every so often as they race to get the Sluagh buried before the sun rises. One more task and we can go home to recover. I refuse to leave anyone behind.

"M'lady," Lucien calls. "The vampires need to get home. It is too close to sunrise."

"You are right, thank you." I turn to say to the vampires in the crowd, "I thank you for your assistance everyone. It looks like all the parts are buried. If you would leave the shovels next to the pile of extra clothes, that would be great. I will contact you when we have a place for a meeting."

I then turn to face the cat shifters and James joins us in his human form. "She is on the second floor and chained with flimsy aluminum-looking chains. She speaks English and was coherent when I saw her, so you can communicate with her. No one gets left behind today."

"I can scale the side of the building with my sai. I bet the smaller cats can too," James offers.

"Wonderful. If you can scale the wall, follow

James and go into the window where I came out. Everyone else can follow me through the ground floor," I say to my feline crowd.

James plunges his sai into the mortar inches above his head and grips the handles. The muscles of his arms and back ripple and strain as he hoists himself up. He repeats the process until he is almost to the window. A line of cats begins to follow him with Nate being the last in the group. I walk toward the front door as James enters the second story window.

I peer into a window on the first floor using a crack between two plywood sheets. Spider webs decorate piles of debris. There are candleholders on the walls, but they are empty of wax. A thick film of dust covers the bits of rock, wood, and the trash littering the floor. This room has not been used in months, perhaps even years. I peer into a second and third window to see identical rooms. I wonder if they never use the bottom floor. Why would that be?

I look over to where Brad is using his massive shoulders to break the plywood covering the door. The lion's head is curled downward, protected by his powerful legs. *Ram! Crack!* The plywood splinters as we breach the first floor. Wood chips fly like shrapnel and everyone on the ground crouches to cover their faces.

I peer between my claws to see a blue light pulsing out of the doorway. It has thrown Brad several feet from the building. The entire building begins to pulse as it starts raining cats upon me. They are being discarded by the wall like a lover throws her clothes on the floor. I turn the other way to see Grant and Gran pulling up in the van.

"Retreat! The van is here. Try to make it to the van." I direct them away from the fortress.

Brad makes it to the van first and almost bowls over Grant who is already opening the door. I pick up a small injured cat in my jaw and run toward the van. Nate picks up another small cat and charges toward the van at my side. We pile into the van like a feline zoo exhibit. I do a quick cat count. Every cat has been rescued but not every member of our team

My heart accelerates. We do not have James in the van. Grant closes us in and awaits my instructions. I'm so used to him taking charge and talking over me, I am surprised by his actions. Perhaps I have earned some respect today. Hope blooms in my chest.

"Where's James?" asks Nate. Everyone presses against the windows to look for him amongst the trees.

"I saw him go inside before the blast," I reply dishearteningly.

"He threw me out of the window as the blast started. I was the only one to reach the top. He's in there alone," says the small cat I had been carrying.

"They must have used the first floor as a trap in case we ambushed them. As soon as I stepped over the threshold, it exploded with black magic," Brad says.

"Then we need to leave now. Black magic is spreading. Look at the grass surrounding the building. It is already dead and decaying. I can't cleanse that much black magic at once and Alison hasn't been trained enough to help me," Gran says while placing her hand on Grant's arm. She squeezes it until I see his jaw prick in irritation. He steps on the gas and the van slowly lumbers to a start.

We ride in uncomfortable silence as the group

wonders if James is all right. We drop off the cats at Bergan to shift and convalesce. We take Gran to Paulino's where we are met by Dr. Van Dijk. He confirms Henrik has a broken leg and it has been set within a temporary cast.

Rosie hugs us all and informs us Henrik is asleep with Anthony and Tommy while Frank Junior watches over them. She tells us to go home so I can recover from my first full shift. Leaving Henrik feels terrifying after watching him being kidnapped but Rosie and Grant are insistent, pushing me into the van.

"Is this as fast as this thing goes?" The van rattles and sputters as it travels over a meadow to the road.

"What do you mean? She's truckin'!" Grant says, smiling to me in the rearview mirror. I smile back shyly. I'm still a giant polar bear. Could my husband be teasing me...as a polar bear? Flirting, when he couldn't stand to be in the same house with human me a few weeks ago?

At my request, we leave the van at the end of our driveway to walk up to the house. It feels heavenly to step on familiar soil. My panic and stress drain into the earth. The positive energy radiates from the earth and warms the chill from my limbs. I take a deep breath to smell the familiar scent of my yard. However, the scent tickling my nose belongs to the male beside me.

Smooth and slightly sweet like a butter cookie, his scent fills my nose, my lungs and the empty places previously filled with fear by the Sluagh. I am instantly aware of his fingertips brushing up and down my spine as we walk into our home.

As we cross the threshold, he turns to me. I allow my eyes to feast upon him as I lift my head to greet his gaze. Powerful legs flank an impressive erection straining the front of his sweatpants. His tight waist widens until his shoulders block out the light from the windows behind him. My claws begin to retract as my fingers itch to touch him. I want to hang from his shoulders while his muscular arms envelop me. I want to feel his lips on mine. I feel desperate to get back to my human form. I use my hind leg to kick the door closed. He reaches over me to lock it and then waits for me to shift.

"Imagine your human form and concentrate on it. Block everything else out. I promise to take care of you, as you took care of me. We are on the same team. I'd like to start again as equals. Stay and let me love you, not rule over you, but actually love you. When I found out you were taken and it was all my fault, I couldn't breathe.

"I didn't just marry you to do the right thing. I married you to be around you forever. You bring life to my world and bring out my fun side. Please stay. Tell me we will manage together. I found out the hard way I can't do it all. I tried to save everyone and in doing so, I almost lost the ones I need most," Grant says with tears in his eyes.

As he speaks, I focus on my human self. I feel my muzzle retract revealing my smaller facial features. My paws narrow into small hands with delicate fingers and shrink to tiny feet. My body aches as the organs decrease in volume and my bones minimize the size of my body cavity. Lastly, the white hairs shrink into my skin, revealing my freckles. In the end, I am perched on my hands and knees in front of Grant.

I feel the fatigue in my body, but it is briskly

pushed aside by a surge of lust. His declaration of love
and promise of partnership lights a fire in me. I shake
my head to clear it, sending my hair flying over my
shoulders. My skin is ultra-sensitive from the shift and
feels foreign to me. I can feel the air move over my
shoulders as Grant's breath becomes ragged. I breathe
deeply just to inhale a lungful of his heady scent.

He steps toward the kitchen and I clasp his pant leg
in my fist. "I don't need comforting right now," I say in
a husky voice that sounds like it belongs to someone
else. I grab at his waistband with my other hand and
rise to my knees. He is staring down at me with wild
eyes.

I slowly lower his pants down to his ankles. I run
my hands over his calves and behind his knees.
Emboldened, I smooth my hands up the back of his
thighs to lightly squeeze his cheeks. I hear him hiss
through his teeth.

I am now at eye level with his sex. My anxiety
chooses this moment to flood me with shyness and look
to him for reassurance. I have never dared to do this
before even though it has played a part in many of my
fantasies. He has thrown his head back so I can't see his
expression. He waits patiently, not suggesting my
course of action with his gaze. His hands hang limply at
his sides, giving me the ultimate gift of trust and
control. "I'm staying. I never thought to leave," I say
breathing directly over him.

I test our boundaries by flicking, licking and
rubbing in different ways. I use his little sounds and
twitches to learn his body responses. I hear his breath
hitch and sputter as I play. Having an extra sensitivity
to mouthfeel and texture makes this act as thrilling for

me as it is for him.

He may see a vixen, but it is a symptom of my disorder that encourages me to pleasure him this way. I stick out my tongue to run it along the length of him forcing a moan from his lips. I'm addicted to the power in giving him so much pleasure. I regret all the distance we have maintained over the years and vow to make up for it. Starting now.

I take each of his hands in mine and guide his fingers through my hair. Each hand instantly turns to fists and the gentle tugging sensation zings through my entire body. I feel my nipples pebble in response, and I moan. The action opens my mouth wide and I slide him into it. I repeat the motion going a little deeper each time, testing my own limits.

I feel his tip hit the back of my throat, causing another zing of electricity to shoot down my body. I apply suction and look up for reassurance. I am scorched by the look of desire in Grant's eyes. I back off until he's almost free and then suck him to the back of my throat, all the while watching his eyes. They cross.

"The first way I'm going to show you respect is not fucking you on the hardwood floor," he says through gritted teeth. He wraps his hands around my waist and flings me over his shoulder. He kicks off his pants and races up the stairs to our bedroom. I laugh as I swing upside down with each step on the staircase. Watching his assets from this angle is almost too much. I'm withdrawn from my eye candy abruptly as I'm thrown onto our bed. My back bounces on impact and I squeal in delight.

I look at his face. My laughter is squelched. Dark

passion haunts his eyes as they devour me whole. My gaze meets his in intensity, balancing the power between us. He lowers his head to my lap to inhale deeply. He lets out a moan as he climbs onto the bed. He looms over me and I brace my hands on his shoulders.

I can't help but press my fingertips into his muscles. He opens his mouth as he lowers his head to mine. I take control of the kiss as soon as our lips meet. Our tongues tangle wildly as I invade his mouth. His hands rise to cup my breasts and feather over my nipples.

"I need more than that," I growl at him. He flips us over easily with his enhanced strength and positions me straddling his stomach. My confidence falters slightly as I am opened and exposed against him. He places a hand on the back of my neck and leans me toward him. I assume he wants to reengage our kiss, but he surprises me place holding my shoulders in place above him. He nips at my chest with his elongated teeth and lays his head down pulling me with him.

The rough treatment breaks through my sensory barriers and a jolt of pleasure zips through my body. A husky moan is released from the bottom of my soul followed by his growl of approval. My apprehension is reduced to a pile of rubble as our emotional baggage is released. I start to see stars and wonder what he's going to do next.

He tugs my arms again and pulls me to a sitting position. I am straddling his face with my core right over his mouth. I start to feel awkward, doing something so wanton. The cool air of the room gives me goosebumps elevating my awareness to my exposed position. He touches me with adoration and reverence, bringing my conscious thought out of my anxiety-ridden spiral. A glance at the tulip on my nightstand clicks it into place. He's holding me like the vase supports the flower. He came to my bed as a shifter with the purpose of dominating me. Using his body like a cage, he demonstrated his previous role in our relationship. He returned today to reaffirm we are alive and together after nearly losing me. However, in this posture, it is not self-doubts that tap-dance over my skin. It is power. It is the power from being rooted securely by a strong partner with the freedom to move my upper body. I look down to thank him for this gift. When our gazes meet, it overwhelms me. My thoughts begin to short-circuit, and I'm lost to the sensation.

I'm barely aware of my subtle hip movements until they send me gently rocking over his face. He growls as he plunders my most secret treasures. My toes curl, my legs tense and my heart pounds. I can feel a fireball traveling up my legs. It threatens to completely unravel me. I panic and start to push him away with feathery hand movements.

"Trust in me. I won't let you hurt anymore, Love," he says to soothe me. He wraps his arm around me and squeezes until I'm lying flat against him. The movement fits us together like perfectly matched puzzle pieces and my heart skips a beat. I can hear myself begging him for release, unable to command my body to do it for myself. He rewards me with a rough open-mouthed kiss. I am overwhelmed with the feeling that we were meant to be together and every trial of our marriage has led to this. We are stronger as a unit than the sum of our two hearts. Something spiritual inside me begins to reach for him without fear of rejection.

As his lovemaking rocks our bodies, a fireball rips through my being. I roar loudly with enough force to shake the walls of our bedroom. My whole body pulses in his arms. My inner walls squeeze him like a vise strangling out his orgasm. He roars in response to mine, a mating of two savage predators. We pulse as a unit for several minutes, enjoying the return to earth.

Boneless and pliant, I allow him to push me to the side. He coils his body around mine and smooths my hair back. He braces me against him with one arm over my body while he invades me with two rough fingers. I feel his teeth as he marks my neck. I instantly orgasm again and pulse in his grip.

Bliss clouds my brain as, for the first time, his soul is claiming mine as a mate. I am his and he is mine. Not just on a piece of paper but in our hearts. We fall happily asleep as a unit, clinging to each other physically but our souls cemented securely.

"Mine," I whisper in the quiet.

Chapter 28

I wait until the sun is fully risen before entering my garden. Someday the apprehension over finding a Sluagh there will go away or perhaps that feeling will keep me alive. Armed with a supply list from Gran, I step into my domain to do what I do best. This Green Witch is going to fight Black magic with Earth magic.

I place a half dozen plastic pots in a row in my largest bed and crouch beside the bed to fill them with dirt. Gran's list calls for hundreds of pounds of Lotus tree leaves while I currently only have one tree. Picking a handful of leaves from the established tree, I set to work making a grove. My task is interrupted by the heavy thumps of Grant's footsteps.

"It's me," he calls, "not a Sluagh."

"Grant," I reply shaking my head, "Sluagh glide over the ground. I would recognize your footsteps anywhere. You have the stealth of a jumbo jet."

"It's part of my charm," he says, joining me at the garden bed. "I brought two cups of coffee and an extra pair of hands. Can I be on your team?"

While Grant has always pulled his weight in our household, I can't help but wonder if he has some residual fear from the kidnapping or residual glow from our bedroom activities last night. "I can manage this if you need to go into the office. Henrik can't help with his injury, but I have Rosie bringing her boys over after lunch. We will find a way; we always do."

"It's Sunday so I should be here with you, not the office."

"That has never stopped you before—"

"I can't pin down when our marriage started to unravel. I let the strands of it slip through my fingers, but I never let go. I have loved you from day one but forgot how to tell you. You put up walls between us...I forgot I was allowed to climb them."

"I don't think either of us was paying attention until it was too late."

"It's still not too late, right?"

"It's not if you are willing to stand beside me, that is if I let down my walls..."

"I made it, Alison. My dreams are realized...thanks to you and all you have sacrificed. I've been a fool to take you for granted. Now is the time to revel in success, where I can choose where I want to be. I choose to be out here with you."

My heart jumps into my mouth as I take in his words. I stop shoveling dirt to turn to him. The love shining in his eyes knocks me off my toes, so I am fully sitting in the grass. The shift in my soul tells me he means this. "It wasn't as much of a sacrifice as you think," I say looking at the ground.

"I used you too. Your persona is so large I have been able to hide in plain view. You have provided a secure place for me to shelter my disability and allowed me to cower in your shadow without pressure. It was not right, but it felt good." I give him a half-smile, letting him see I am as guilty as he was in letting our marriage fall apart.

"I am fascinated by you and all your quirks, do you

know that?"

"You have never made me feel strange. It's what I love most about you."

"It's more than acceptance and I think that's the piece I haven't conveyed fully. I love the way your mind works. You see the world in an intense array of colors most people cannot even sense. I want to experience life through your eyes. It is not enough to watch you, to have you anymore. Please let me into your world," he says taking my hands in his grip.

I can only nod in return as my tears choke the words I try to say. This is the partnership I have always wanted but never felt I deserved. I concentrate on the pressure of his hands over mine. I am not dreaming. Even if this is a reality, Grant has always had a silver tongue. How can I trust he is not feeding me lip service?

As if reading my mind he says, "I know. I know. You don't believe my words. I still remember you saying my words no longer carry weight with you. However, will you give me time to prove it? Can I demonstrate to the commander of an animal shifter pack I deserve to be her chosen mate? That I can stand beside you and not in front of you?"

"Grant," I say breathlessly, "I would love to be your partner. I will need your guidance as I take on a leadership role. I will need your strength as I lead the pack against the Fae. I will need your support as I balance it all. Most of all I will need your love, I don't think I can do it without the ability to recuperate in your care."

"I live to provide for you—"

"You never have failed at providing, Grant. If we

work together, I believe we can be greater than the sum of our two selves. Let's try being married as equals."

"Then let me help," he says, placing a lotus leaf in my palm. Together we reach inside the first pot of dirt, sinking our entwined fingers beneath the surface. I inhale in to draw the power of the Earth through our bodies and exhale to stimulate the leaf. Grant's breathing matches mine and his heartbeat slows to my tempo. He closes his eyes to bask in his first taste of my magic. The next breath pushes roots from the stalk of the leaf. One more breath pushes a neophyte to breach the surface of the dirt. With each successive breath, the stem thickens into a trunk and a tree grows until it towers over our heads.

"See our love is pretty magical," I say removing our hands from the dirt. I try to remove my hand from his, but he holds it firmly.

"The magic comes from you," he whispers. He glides the fingertips of his free hand along my hairline. As if on autopilot, I lean into his hand until he has cupped my jaw. The chaste kiss he intends to give me lights my heart on fire. I kiss him with all my power to relieve the need for him building within my soul. Within minutes, we are gasping for air looking into each other's eyes with longing.

"How long have you known?"

"Only as long as I have been a shifter. Ironically, I was lurking in the trees trying to brainstorm how I was going to tell you magic exists and I had been changed. You already knew everything I wanted to say but hadn't let me in on the secret."

"I'm sorry I didn't tell you. I was so grateful you accepted my SPD that I didn't want to push my luck with telling I was a witch too. I was born as a witch so the two secrets to my strangeness go hand-in-hand. My family knows and have helped me keep the secret since I was a kid—"

"Not all of your family, not when I didn't know. I want to be included in your inner circle like you want to be included in the community. I have a different way of expressing it," he says. I am shocked by his display at vulnerability. Perhaps he has changed after all. This is the olive branch I have been seeking. The branch we will use to build a sturdier foundation.

I take his hand and we create a second tree, then a third, then a fourth. "I have much more energy when I am connected with you. Usually, I would need to rest between trees. Thank you for lending your strength," I whisper. The breath is swept from my lungs as I take in his beaming smile. The dimples at the corners of his mouth wink at me while his eyes sparkle.

"I am going to need the support of the entire pack to rescue James and I don't know how to ask for it," I say after we grow the last tree. I pull him to standing and we stroll back to the herb gardens to harvest basil, white sage, osmanthus, and rosehips for Gran's black magic potion.

"Well, in the pharma business, when you need people you have a meeting. Not only can I give you strength for garden magic, but I teach you to create business magic. In fact, I already started," he says, withdrawing my phone from his pocket.

When I frown at him he adds, "it has a gift inside. I installed the Bergan Pharma all-call system on it and had Nate add you to the permissions roster this morning. With a click of a button, you can contact all of

Bergan, the board of directors or just the shifters. You don't need me to contact them for you. You are in command."

I am shocked to my toes. Grant finally has total control of a pharma company after following the orders of those who don't know the business for all of his career, and he is giving it to me. I sit open mouthed as he places the phone into my hands and starts explaining the app Nate created. His oath of fealty to me at the Sluagh castle was not a gesture. He coaches me through calling a meeting for tomorrow night and together, we get back to fulfilling Gran's herbal list. With Grant at my side, I will have the strength to lead the Strawberry Shifters pack.

Chapter 29

"Are you sure I look okay?"

"Alison, you look great in that suit. Stop tugging on it. Wait, are you wearing shoes? You are but they are on the wrong feet. You might want to correct them before you start talking about your vision for the pack," Rosie says while shaking her head.

"Thank you," I say to my shoes. Being touch under-receptive, I don't feel the difference in my left and right shoes. These pumps do not have stickers in them to label the correct foot. Ugh, grown-up shoes.

"And Rosie, thank you for all your help to set up my first pack meeting. I plan to stick as close to Frankie's procedures as possible and I couldn't have done it without you. You are the best friend I have wanted my whole adult life."

"It's my pleasure, Madam Commander."

"Oh, do you have to call me that? It sounds so severe and formal," I say tugging at my velvet blazer. I wanted to look professional, so I dusted off my old interviewing suit. When I couldn't wedge a blouse underneath it, I tried to borrow another blazer from Rosie. Instead, I got wolf whistles and encouragement to stay as I am.

"Commander is who you are, Flower," says Gran from Paulino's dining room entrance. "I am delighted to watch whether you will grow into the title or the title will grow with you. We have not met as a whole pack since my son passed away. Please be sensitive to that."

"—And don't worry about the dinner," Rosie says, jumping in. "Everyone will gather around you to say their piece before sitting down to eat. Once they start eating, they won't watch you."

"I hadn't planned on eating in front of anyone," I say with a band of anxiety forming over my ribs. The squeeze chokes my last word, so it is released as a squeak.

"You will learn. My food is too good to resist," Rosie says with a wink.

"About that, I may have already had my first blunder inviting the vampires to a family dinner when they don't eat and have never been included in the family."

"If you choose to include them, I guess you have good reasons," Rosie says with a raised eyebrow.

"I am forever grateful to Ryan for bringing Grant to the Sluagh fortress—"

"—and having a fistfight with him instead of rescuing you?"

"Maybe not that part, but he did look out for me before I knew there was danger."

"Look out for you or look at you. Girl, he keeps binoculars on his deck—facing your house. Don't get me started on the view inside those giant windows of yours."

"Giving Ryan and the vampires a chance feels like the right thing to do. I may regret it later, but I can't turn my back on help. They buried Sluagh parts under my command. They can't be all bad."

"Well, I think you invited trouble between Ryan

and Grant by having them in the same room. Brainstorm a way to keep them apart."

"Grant said he will support my decisions. So here is his chance," I say in my teacher's voice. Inside I am a boiling cauldron of nervousness. Can the vampires and shifters maintain their harmony if I force them to work closely together? Perhaps I should have asked Brad for the working relationship between the two groups. No, I don't want to start my tenure with prejudging half the town. Everyone deserves a chance.

"Flower visualize the meeting and tell me what you need," Gran says in her cryptic voice. She reserves this voice for her visions and the hairs on my arms raise in alarm.

I close my eyes and see myself at the front of the room. Grant barrels into my imagination and takes over, physically removing me from the lectern. I see pack members rushing me at the end, tapping my shoulder to get my attention. They turn away in disgust when I don't respond. I can't feel the taps. My horror ends when I snap my eyes open. Gran and Rosie are looking at me with concerned expressions.

"Rosie, how do I keep people from touching me?"

"Uh, your husband is a mean grizzly so that should take care of it…"

"Grant too," I say, "how can I hold my space, so I physically have control over the room?"

"Every commander needs a fortress," says Gran as she points her cane at the stack of extra chairs.

****

"This is the last time I walk anywhere. I am ordering a car tomorrow and Bergan is going to pay for it," I grouse to Nate as we walk to Paulino's pizzeria.

"You will have to get the okay from the big boss," replies Nate.

"Brad went over Bergan's financials with me today. Even without Julibamar coming online, our company has more money than we can spend in our extended lifetimes," I say, holding the door open.

"Not Brad," Nate snickers as I open the door, "I meant the really big boss. You know, the one who controls the money, the people, and the access to pizza." We are greeted by the scents of garlic and herbs. Even though Paulino's is closed, it seems Rosie and the boys have been cooking.

There is a steady stream of people entering the pizza place. Earlier in the day, Alison had sent out an all-call text inviting us to a "lessons learned" meeting. As I walk down the gauntlet, I hear the soft din of people filling the dining room.

I turn the corner by the hostess sign and notice the buffet tables set up at the back of the room. My stomach rumbles loudly and the clump of people gathered at the opening to the room begins to laugh quietly.

"Watch out, Papa Bear spies food!" Nate jokes. The whole room laughs at my expense and I graciously put my hand over my stomach to take a mock bow. I cannot pull the attention away from Alison in any way. If I bulldoze her, she will think I haven't kept my word to be her partner and not her handler.

****

Even with the murmur of the crowd filling the dining room, my ears focus on the thundering footsteps of Grant's approach. My senses tune toward the gauntlet and my heart begins to pound. Torn between the excitement to see him and the dread of having to share a spotlight with him, my insides are churning.

A soon as he passes the hostess stand, there is a commotion. My confidence deflates as the heads in the room turn toward him in unison. The crowd laughs and Nate plays the sidekick with a pithy comment. Doubts fill my head and the room begins to spin. How did I expect this to go?

My gaze darts across the room where Rosie is stacking glasses by the soda fountain. She touches her throat and nods at me. My friend is right. I need to find my voice. My teacher's voice is waiting for my confidence to emerge instead of taking control. It starts with one small centering breath. I build a spark of positive energy in my chest. A second breath is slightly larger and grows the spark into a flame. Warmth radiates from it and my limbs stop shaking. A third breath lifts my chin and clears my facial expression.

****

"We will go over our business first, followed by a family meal just like Frankie's meetings," my wife's voice calls from the front of the room. She has a ring of chairs set up around her workspace facing outward to keep people from crowding too closely and making her sensory issues flare. She looks like an exhibit at an art museum, a living doll. I'm drawn to her like a magnet. I'm halfway across the room before I realize I have physically moved.

The soft glow of the table lamps luminesces her pale skin giving her the look of porcelain. The angles of her jaw and cheekbones are highlighted since her hair is secured at the base of her head. I envision my hands removing that barrette and fanning her hair over our pillows. As my pants start to feel smaller, I decide to sit and focus on something other than her hair. Bad. Move.

She is wearing a black velvet blazer with very little underneath it. My mark on her neck peeks out from the collar every time she bends her elbows. I feel a warmth in my chest swell with pride and ownership. She steps on a cord accidentally, turns and bends down to plug it back in. I get a few seconds of her mouthwatering curves encased in a black velvet skirt. I'm enjoying the view when I become conscious of the fact we have an audience.

I glare at everyone whose head is turned in her direction. A growl resonates from me before I can stop it. Alison straightens abruptly and smiles my way. The growl instantly stops because my heart stops. Even though she is about to address the entire town, she takes a moment to comfort me.

****

If this meeting lasts more than an hour, I'm kicking these pumps to the corner. How do they help me look professional when they get caught on every cord and carpet rut? Getting the heel caught on my laptop cord has unplugged it again. Now I have the delay of its reboot. My only saving grace is it is a state-of-the-art piece of technology gifted to me from Grant.

While I right the errant plug, a growl rumbles in my direction. If I get one more catcall or wolf-whistle from this group of shifters, I'm going to...the growl came from Grant. Leering eyes drop to their laps as the men ogling my backside bow to the predator seated in the audience.

I can't help my beaming smile. Grant is protecting me from afar. He has my back, literally in this case, but hasn't breached my fortress. I'm still in control while he is in the audience. He gets it. I have his support without hiding behind him.

****

"Hey, why do we have the mood lighting? I can turn on the overhead lights. I'm right by the switch," Nate says loudly.

He stops as a chorus of growls comes from behind him. Ray has entered the room while pushing Matteo in a wheelchair. They are followed by the rest of Rosie's boys and they are all growling. Their eyes glow yellow and they bare their teeth.

"She likes the lighting soft, so the lighting is soft," Matteo says from his wheelchair. His voice and presence give off the impression of a seasoned warrior, not a twelve-year-old kid. He has both of his legs and one arm in a cast. He will endure more than one surgery in his recovery from fighting the Sluagh.

I will always be grateful to the kid who defended my wife before the ultimate monster. Nate looks from one member of the wolf pack to another. He shrugs and drops his hand from the switch nonchalantly. Only those who spend as much time with him as I do would recognize this as a retreat. Rosie has raised a formidable little army. I'm pleased they have already shown their fealty to Alison.

Behind the Paulino boys, the vampire leaders saunter into the dining room carrying sunglasses in their hands. They approach Alison's makeshift barricade and she greets them before they try to breach it. I bite the inside of my cheek as each one bows to kiss her hand. I draw blood in my mouth when I see her smiling and talking to them.

****

"We can't tell you how much we appreciate your inclusion of us. We were surprised by your invitation," Ryan says while holding my hand in his icy clutches. I shake my hand loose to tuck a strand of hair behind my ear that has escaped my ponytail. I use the action to sneak a glance at Grant. He is watching from his seat in the audience. Will he let me handle this or be a bulldozer?

"Thank you for keeping the lights low too," David adds, leading the trio to put their sunglasses in pockets in unison. "It is nice to be able to enjoy this room without sunglasses."

"Of course, I would include you," I say, "not only did you watch out for me personally, but you helped the pack with my rescue. You are a part of this town and we are grateful for your help."

"We are usually left out because we are not shifters. We require extra steps to feel comfortable because we are not like everyone else," Ryan says.

"Please tell me those extra needs and I will do my best to make it a comfortable environment for all. I empathize with your need to have accommodations," I say gesturing to my barrier. The vampires smile making their centered irises bounce like playground balls. Having reversed iris-pupil eyes must make them extremely light-sensitive.

"Being different is no reason to be left out," Henrik interjects as he wobbles on his crutches to sit next to the barrier. "If a plant doesn't grow, we don't throw out the plant. We change its environment until it thrives. Right, Mom?"

"That's right. Oh no! Is the smell of garlic making

you ill?" Not only do they not eat but I have invited them into a noxious cloud of garlic. They must think I am a bungling assassin. I hope they see my gestures are inclusion and not initiation of war.

"No, we can even eat it. The aversion to garlic thing is part of the folktale lore surrounding us," Ryan says as the vampires take their seats. I sigh in relief as they turn their backs to me. Rosie says the posture is a shifter's way of announcing fealty. Perhaps it is the same with vampires. I will have to ask Gran if there is a vampire etiquette book in existence.

****

I watch Alison close her eyes and take a deep breath. She does this a lot before her strength shines through. She opens her eyes and focuses on me. I smile at her and nod. I hope she knows it means I'm on her team. When she smiles in response, I feel my throat tighten with emotion.

"Let's get started, please," she projects, "I'm going to pass around this clipboard with a sign-up sheet. If you would please fill in your name, your power animal, and your previous battle assignments under Frankie. Also, there is a spot for where you are employed so I know if you are already on the all-call text list or if I need to add you. Just put BP for Bergan Pharmaceuticals in the small box, if that is applicable.

"While it is circulating, we would usually start our meeting with our financial status and potential Sluagh sighting followed by lessons learned during our first battle. However, I think a moment of silence to commemorate Frankie should be first."

She clasps her small hands at her waist and tips her head forward. Like a theater curtain, strands of red hair slide forward to obscure her features. The members of the audience bow their heads too. Brad closes his eyes and slowly squeezes and releases his hands. I look over to Rosie who is clinging to her boys and passing out tissues. The only sounds are the younger boys crying openly into their older brothers' shirts. Matteo is clenching his jaw so hard I fear he will grind his teeth to stumps.

"Thank you," Alison says somberly. "It still isn't back to business. Bear with me, but we have a crisis. James and an unknown woman with golden hair are currently locked inside the Sluagh fortress by some black magic force. She told me at the next new moon a large flock of Sluagh will be exiled to the fortress.

"The General and Sargent, defeated in my rescue, were test subjects. I believe the Fae will consider their extermination a free service provided by us, and actually be more motivated to send their undesirables here. So tonight, it is imperative we devise a rescue plan which we will execute tomorrow. We cannot delay in retrieving them," Alison begins.

Brad raises his hand and Alison acknowledges him. "Do you already have a plan? When will we get our battle assignments before tomorrow?"

"Since I was isolated from you for my only battle with the Sluagh and there are no written records on your previous battles, I want to create a battle plan as a group. Everyone will leave here with a clear understanding of their role tonight. It is only as a group that we are powerful enough to defeat the Fae."

Alison pauses to take another deep breath. Once she has gathered her strength, she asks, "more questions?" She stands with her arms crossed and scans the crowd. The room is so quiet you could hear a pin drop.

"Great, then I would like to start with Gran giving us an explanation for the blue light radiating out of the fortress…"

I am enraptured by her sweet yet formidable presence. The whole town is working together under her leadership. She commands the room without yelling, threatening or fighting with anyone.

She was born for this role and I almost sabotaged it by using her condition as an excuse to doubt her. Henrik was right when he said a flower grows when its environment is optimal. It is my job to do this for Alison and I always put my all into my job.

****

To my utter shock, Grant remains quietly seated for the rest of the meeting. With every challenge from the elders, he allowed me to handle them. I am so grateful to have the space to lead without his shadow looming over me. I'm hopeful we have entered a new chapter where we live as equals. He will still rule the pharmaceutical world but now I will feel worthy of sitting at his side.

As the pack members sign up for Black Magic Cleanup with Gran, I get a quiet moment to breathe before the dreaded dinner. As much as I hate eating in front of people, I must go outside of my comfort zone to belong. The dimmed lights and chair fortress are the Paulinos' steps toward compromise. The rest is up to me. Grant helps guide Henrik to a tiny table partially blocked by my ring of chairs.

"Thanks for coordinating James's rescue instead of having a getting-to-know-you powwow," Nate says.

His movements are so quiet I didn't hear him approach. He makes half the sound of Grant despite being several inches taller.

"I value everyone in Strawberry, including the woman chained in the fortress," I say diplomatically.

"James is my best friend. I want you to know I will do anything to get him back."

The jokester has glassy eyes and a sunken posture at the loss of his friend. "I won't let you down," I say, reaching for his hand. I gaze into his elongated pupils and reassure the cat within him. I will save his friend.

He nods in response and trudges to the buffet. My breath hitches. I reached for him to placate his fears in front of Grant. His jealous streak is going to blow a hole through the pizzeria if he saw it.

I make my way to Henrik's table to await Grant's explosion. "Have you seen your Dad?"

"He got my plate and his first one. He is coming over. Right behind you," Henrik says between bites of pizza.

I turn to see Grant with a plate piled high with salad and a large bowl. Despite watching my exchange with Nate, there is no aggression in his posture. He offers the bowl to me with a shy smile. Obscured by the high rim of the bowl are tiny ramekins separating small portions of foods.

Had I approached the buffet table, I would have had an audience. They would have seen my need to separate the textures I eat. I don't need to pick them apart at the table with the smaller containers. My clever husband has diverted the attention to himself. He has learned the balance of taking the spotlight when I need it but letting me shine as well.

"Thank you," I say, covering his hands with my own on the bowl. We stare into each other's eyes with love radiating from our exchange. Hope fills my heart. With Grant at my side, I can fit into this community. If I tell him my needs, he will listen. Our joined souls tell me so.

"Will you dine with us, Madam Commander?" His eyes shine with love as flirtation curls at the corner of his lips.

"Of course, this is exactly where I belong."

A word about the author...

Marilyn Barr currently resides in the wilds of Kentucky with her husband, son, and rescue cats. When engaging with the real world, she is collecting characters, empty coffee cups, and unused homeschool curricula.

She has a diverse background containing experiences as a child prodigy turned medical school reject, biodefense microbiologist, high school science teacher, homeschool mother of a savant, and advocate for the autistic community.

She would love to hear from readers via her website:

www.marilynbarr.com.

Thank you for purchasing
this publication of The Wild Rose Press, Inc.

For questions or more information
contact us at
info@thewildrosepress.com.

The Wild Rose Press, Inc.
www.thewildrosepress.com